Phoenix Television Tell-All

Mailbag

Q. Is it possible that the sizzling sexpot who played Vanessa Vance on the juicy nighttime soap opera *Skin Deep* is alive and well and living in our city's midst? I'm a big fan of *Heads Up*, the nationally syndicated talk show filmed here in Phoenix, Arizona, and I swear I saw Phoebe Lane (Vanessa's *real* name) in the show's credits, as makeup artist. Could it be the same leggy blonde—and is she single?

A. It's true—the knockout Phoebe Lane has turned in her SAG card and is working off camera, applying some cosmetic tricks she learned on those Hollywood sets. You might also be surprised to know that Ms. Lane is a bombshell and an egghead, meaning she's studying biochemistry at Arizona State University—and the curvy lady is setting the *class* curve. But she doesn't spend every night with her books.... Though Ms. Lane swears she's "single and loving it," she's been spotted cozying up with Wyatt Madison, producer of *Heads Up*. Looks as if Ms. Lane may be living her very own soap opera, right here in Phoenix—dating an older man who also happens to be her boss!

P.S. Don't miss *Kiss a Handsome Stranger* by Jacqueline Diamond, available next month from Harlequin American Romance.

Dear Reader,

Spring is the perfect time to celebrate the joy of romance. So get set to fall in love as Harlequin American Romance brings you four new spectacular books.

First, we're happy to welcome *New York Times* bestselling author Kasey Michaels to the Harlequin American Romance family. She inaugurates TEXAS SHEIKHS, our newest in-line continuity, with *His Innocent Temptress.* This four-book series focuses on a Texas family with royal Arabian blood who must fight to reunite their family and reclaim their rightful throne.

Also, available this month, *The Virgin Bride Said,"Wow!"* by Cathy Gillen Thacker, a delightful marriage-of-convenience story and the latest installment in THE LOCKHARTS OF TEXAS miniseries. Kara Lennox provides fireworks as a beautiful young woman who's looking for Mr. Right sets out to *Tame an Older Man* following the advice of 2001 WAYS TO WED, a book guaranteed to provide satisfaction! And *Have Baby, Need Beau* says it all in Rita Herron's continuation of her wonderful THE HARTWELL HOPE CHESTS series.

Enjoy April's selections and come back next month for more love stories filled with heart, home and happiness from Harlequin American Romance.

Wishing you happy reading,

Melissa Jeglinski
Associate Senior Editor
Harlequin American Romance

TAME AN OLDER MAN

Kara Lennox

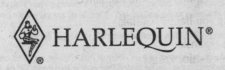

HARLEQUIN®

TORONTO • NEW YORK • LONDON
AMSTERDAM • PARIS • SYDNEY • HAMBURG
STOCKHOLM • ATHENS • TOKYO • MILAN • MADRID
PRAGUE • WARSAW • BUDAPEST • AUCKLAND

Special thanks and acknowledgment are given
to Kara Lennox for her contribution to the
2001 WAYS TO WED series.

For Joseph Preece, a terrific father-in-law.
Thank you for making me feel so welcome.

ISBN 0-373-16871-3

TAME AN OLDER MAN

ABOUT THE AUTHOR

Texas native Kara Lennox has been an art director, typesetter, advertising copy writer, textbook editor and reporter. She's worked in a boutique and a health club, and has conducted telephone surveys. She's been an antiques dealer and briefly ran a clipping service. But no work has made her happier than writing romance novels.

When Kara isn't writing, she indulges in an ever-changing array of weird hobbies, from rock climbing to crystal digging. But her mind is never far from her stories. Just about anything can send her running to her computer to jot down a new idea for some future novel.

Books by Kara Lennox

HARLEQUIN AMERICAN ROMANCE

840—VIRGIN PROMISE
856—TWIN EXPECTATIONS
871—TAME AN OLDER MAN

When three best friends need advice on finding that perfect love match, they turn to the wisest relationship book around, *2001 Ways To Wed*.

Chapter 14
The Mystique of the Older Man

What *is* it about an older man that intrigues us? His debonair demeanor? That irresistible wisp of gray at his temples? The rich life experiences he has to share?

Actually, it's all these—and more. The "December" man may think a "May" woman is a prize—a bit of a trophy. But honestly, it is the distinguished, mature bachelor who is the *lady's* conquest.

What do I mean? Well, this is a man who has held fast to his single lifestyle for decades, turning his back on any relationship that dared to get too close to commitment. Then a fresh-faced female comes along, and wham! Before he knows it, he's on his honeymoon. He didn't just *happen* to relinquish his seat in the Bachelors' Hall of Fame. He was tamed by a younger woman....

Chapter One

Phoebe Lane knocked on her downstairs neighbor's door. The sound of multi-cat yowling greeted her from the other side. "Frannie?" she called. "You home?"

"One minute, one minute," Frannie called. "I'd probably scare you if I came to the door naked, now, wouldn't I?" A moment later the door opened, and Frannie welcomed Phoebe with a smile and slightly bleary eyes. Her red beehive pouf of hair was a little flat on one side and not quite as perky as usual.

"Oh, Frannie, I'm sorry, I didn't mean to get you out of bed."

"That's okay, hon, come on in before the cats get out." She dragged Phoebe in by the elbow. The cats—Phoebe saw at least six—had no intention of escaping. They knew where their meal ticket was. They followed Frannie with adoring eyes and twitching tails, as she led Phoebe into the kitchen and put the coffee on. "I needed to get up, anyway, and feed my babies."

Frannie managed to hold the coffeepot under the tap with one hand while pouring dry cat food into several pet bowls with the other. Phoebe could only hope Frannie didn't get mixed up and put cat food in the coffeemaker.

"What's got you up so early on a Saturday morning?" Frannie asked.

"It's our new neighbor. His car is in the carport, so he must be home for a change. I was hoping I could get a look at him. I bet we can see his balcony from your patio."

Frannie's eyes sparkled. "The mysterious, reclusive Wyatt Madison. Why can't you spy on his balcony from the courtyard?"

"I can't see his balcony through those overachiever palm trees growing from your patio," Phoebe explained.

"And what makes you think Mr. Madison will come out on his balcony this particular morning?"

"'Cause the weather's nice?" Phoebe sagged a bit. "All right, so it's not a great plan. Got a better one?"

"Hmm." Frannie distributed the cat food among her herd of felines, her brow furrowed in thought. Then she smiled. "Ah, I know. This will be great."

Phoebe watched, curious, as Frannie selected among her pets one half-grown Siamese kitten. She picked it up and cuddled it, though it protested at being taken away from the food. "Igor loves to climb trees, don't you, baby?" She grabbed a can of cat treats from the top of the refrigerator and headed toward the back of her apartment. "Follow me."

Phoebe couldn't wait to see what her resourceful neighbor had planned. Frannie made it a point to know everything about everybody who lived in Mesa Blue, their condo complex. But Wyatt Madison, who was house-sitting while his grandparents were away on a month-long cruise, had proved quite a challenge. *No one* had seen him. All they knew about him was that he'd moved recently from Chicago to Phoenix to produce a nationally syndicated talk show, "Heads Up," and that his grandparents thought he walked on water.

"You'll be sweet to Wyatt, won't you?" 80-year-old Helen Madison had asked, as Phoebe helped her with the last-minute packing for her European cruise, the vacation she and her husband Rolland had planned for years. "He's such a dear, but he needs some, er, female guidance, if you know what I mean."

Precisely the reason Phoebe was so curious about the man.

"You know," Frannie said as she led the way through the living room and to her large patio, where a couple more cats lazed in the sun, "I don't blame you for trying to meet Wyatt before any of the other girls in this building get their hooks in him. It's about time you took an interest in romance."

Phoebe laughed. "I'm *not* interested in romance with Wyatt Madison. Please!" She'd sworn off men for the foreseeable future.

"Don't knock it 'til you've tried it," Frannie said, batting her eyelashes. "Nothing makes a woman feel young and gorgeous like an attentive man. Of course, I guess that doesn't apply to you. You're already young and gorgeous."

"It's the burden I live with," Phoebe quipped, though she was half serious.

"Anyway, if you're not out to jump his bones—"

"I'm just curious, Frannie," Phoebe said with a laugh. Actually, she *was* interested in Wyatt's romantic potential. But not for herself. One of her best friends, Daisy Redford, who lived on the second floor, had a ticking biological clock. Phoebe and her other best friend, Elise Foster, had pledged to help Daisy find her man. They were leaving no stone unturned—even if it meant going along with some wacky scheme of Frannie's.

Frannie stood at the back of the patio, set the cat down, opened the can of cat treats, and let Igor have a sniff. "Yummy, yummy," she said. Then she took a morsel from the can and lobbed it up toward the third floor—toward Wyatt's balcony.

"You aren't serious!" Phoebe said, laughing. "This won't work!"

"Just watch."

It took her a few tries, but Frannie had an admirable hook shot. Eventually a piece of the treat actually landed on Wyatt's balcony. And the cat, watching carefully, saw it.

Frannie held the cat next to the trunk of a palm tree that grew straight up from her patio to the third floor. Igor immediately got the idea. He sank his claws into the tree and, with his goal firmly in mind, started to climb.

"How did you know he would do that?" Phoebe asked.

"Like I said, Igor loves climbing trees. He also *always* gets stuck. Now we have a perfect excuse to knock on the mysterious Mr. Madison's door."

Phoebe and Frannie watched long enough to feel certain the sure-footed feline would complete his mission, then scurried up to the third floor themselves, though they chose to use the stairs.

Phoebe's heart thumped as they approached Wyatt's door. "This is kind of dishonest, don't you think?"

"Of course not. The cat *is* stuck, or he will be shortly. How else would I get him down?" Frannie stopped before the door and knocked smartly.

"Who is it?" a deep, oddly muffled-sounding voice asked from the other side.

"It's your neighbors, Frannie and Phoebe," Frannie said brightly.

"Come on in," the voice beckoned. "Door's unlocked."

Frannie didn't hesitate. Phoebe followed her inside, and both of them looked around for the source of the voice.

"Mr. Madison?" Frannie called.

"In the kitchen."

The women followed the sound of the voice into the kitchen, and Phoebe stifled a gasp as she laid eyes on the most delightful set of male buns she'd ever seen. It quickly became apparent why Wyatt's voice had been muffled. He had his head and shoulders buried under the kitchen sink.

"I'm right in the middle of something," he said, pleasantly enough. "If I let go, I'll flood the whole kitchen. Can I help you?"

Frannie, her gaze riveted on that wonderful butt covered with snug, faded denim, couldn't seem to articulate an answer. Phoebe jumped in.

"We're really sorry to bother you, but Frannie's cat seems to have climbed up a tree by your balcony, and now he's stuck. We thought you could get him down for us.''

''I, um, can't right now.'' Wyatt seemed to be wrestling with a stubborn pipe or something. His muscles bulged as he applied pressure to a wrench. The wrench slipped. ''Ouch. Damn it! Um, 'scuse me.''

''How long do you think you'll be?''

''At the rate I'm going? Hours. Why don't you go on back to my balcony and see if you can get the cat yourself?''

That wasn't the plan! Phoebe looked at Frannie, who shrugged helplessly. ''I guess we can try,'' Phoebe said. With luck, the cat would be too high or too low for them to reach.

Phoebe tried to take everything in, searching for clues to Wyatt's personality as she and Frannie headed for the French doors that led out to the balcony. But the apartment looked almost identical to the way it had before the elder Madisons had left—tastefully decorated, accented with a few souvenirs from their travels around the world. Wyatt hadn't put much of a stamp on the place.

When they stepped outside, a veritable jungle of plants greeted them. Helen had quite the green thumb, and she nurtured everything from ferns to cacti on her roomy terrace. They all looked happy and healthy, as if Wyatt was taking good care of them. He probably was, too, knowing how unhappy Helen would be if any of her darlings expired during her vacation.

Phoebe noticed a couple of new additions, two huge potted cactus plants. Then she spotted Igor perched in the top of a palm tree—at shoulder level, perfectly within reach of either woman. *Rats.* He mewed pitifully, and Frannie plucked him out of the tree and cuddled him. "Oh, poor baby. Mama played a mean trick on you, didn't she, pushing you up that tree when she knew you'd get stuck. Let's go home and get a treat."

"I guess we can't linger out here without arousing suspicion," Phoebe agreed.

They stopped in the kitchen on the way out. Wyatt was still busily engaged with his plumbing. Well, at least they'd discovered he had a nice rear and a pleasant voice.

"Did you get the cat?" he asked.

"Yes," Frannie said. "May I bring you some brownies to thank you?"

"I didn't really do anything. Anyway, I'm allergic to chocolate, but thanks."

Frannie and Phoebe looked at each other, but they were both out of ideas. "Well, guess we'll leave," Phoebe said. "Unless you need help with that plumbing?"

"Got it covered, thanks."

They left. "Mission failed," Phoebe murmured as she bid Frannie goodbye at the top of the stairs.

WYATT JUST LAY THERE under the sink for a few moments after the two women left. He'd been dying to get a look at the young one, Phoebe. He knew she was young because his grandparents had spoken endlessly of how beautiful she was, how nice, and how single. It was no secret they wanted him safely married off and providing them with great-grandchildren.

He'd always thought he wanted to get married

someday, but someday had never come. He was thirty-nine but still in no hurry, not when he was on such a crucial rung of his career ladder, working sixteen-hour days to get "Heads Up" off on the right foot. He especially wasn't interested in a platinum-blond beauty. The pretty ones were always trouble, their motives never to be trusted.

Still, Phoebe's voice had sent pleasurable chills up his spine. He couldn't be blamed for wanting to look.

When the plumbing job was finally finished, Wyatt took a moment to admire his handiwork. The kitchen faucet now ran hot and cold water at an appropriate volume without flooding the countertop. Satisfied, he grabbed a bottle of fruit juice as a reward and headed for his balcony. Since his move to Phoenix, he'd been stuck in the studio night and day. Now that he finally had a day off, he could appreciate the fine spring weather. What a switch it was from Chicago!

He sat down in one of the deck chairs and took a draw on his O.J. But relaxing didn't come easy to him. Never had. First he saw some brown leaves on one of his grandmother's ferns that had to be pinched. Then a spot of something orange on the balcony decking caught his eye. He picked up the small, soft, orange lump and sniffed it.

Smelled like fish. Cat food. Uh-huh.

Apparently Miss Phoebe felt the need for subterfuge in getting into his apartment. Apparently she believed that just introducing herself was too obvious.

He sighed, disappointed. Though why should Phoebe Lane be any different from every other attractive woman he met? It wouldn't matter how subtle her machinations. He couldn't, wouldn't, get her on TV.

RATHER THAN TRAIPSING back to her own apartment two doors down from Wyatt's, Phoebe went down to the second floor and knocked on Elise's door.

"Come in, it's unlocked," Elise called. That seemed to be the policy around Mesa Blue. Everybody knew everybody—except Wyatt, of course—and since access to the building was controlled by twenty-four-hour security, the building had become its own small town. That was one of the reasons Phoebe had decided to move here. Her grandmother had left the condo to her in her will. Surprised and grateful—Phoebe had scarcely ever met her father's mother—she welcomed the opportunity to flee Hollywood and settle into Mesa Blue's warm, friendly environs.

She entered Elise's apartment to find her friend lounging on her sofa reading a *Bride* magazine and sipping coffee. Her light brown hair was up in a ponytail, and she wore gym shorts and a T-shirt, looking as if she'd just finished an exercise routine.

Elise smiled a welcome. "Hey, get some coffee and sit down."

Phoebe did just that. She loved Elise's apartment, with its comfy furniture and its eclectic collection of books, pictures and plants. It was the sort of apartment a college professor should live in, which was only fitting, since that's what Elise was. She taught French at Arizona State University.

Phoebe was sad that Elise would be moving out when she got married in a few months, though happy her friend had found such a wonderful man in James Dillon.

"Any progress in checking out Wyatt Madison?" Elise asked.

"That's why I'm here. I've failed miserably. Although I can tell you he has a butt to die for."

Elise's eyebrows flew up. "Oh, really?"

"And a nice voice."

"Maybe I shouldn't ask."

"He had his head stuck under the sink, for gosh sake," Phoebe said. "Even Frannie couldn't lure him out. We've got to come up with a plan."

Elise set aside the magazine. "In that case..." She hopped up, went to her bookcase, and after a moment's perusal selected a large white paperback with blue lettering.

"Why didn't I think of that?" Phoebe said with a laugh, as Elise resumed her seat and started flipping through the book, *2001 Ways to Wed* by Jane Jasmine. The book was a surprise hit with women all over the country, women who previously thought they were doomed to a life of loneliness. From Seattle to Miami, they claimed Ms. Jasmine's eminently sensible advice had helped them find husbands.

Actually, Elise was one of those women, although she hadn't actually been looking for a husband when she'd found James. She'd only been looking for a temporary escort to take her to a family wedding and *pretend* to be her fiancé. She'd sought out someone in the Drama Department at the university, a professor who could act the part of a devoted fiancé, and had found a millionaire, instead.

"This book actually has some wonderful advice," Elise said.

"Any advice for luring a workaholic recluse from his lair?" Phoebe asked. "I swear, if the Madisons didn't insist he was such a catch—so absolutely perfect—I wouldn't bother with him."

"There's a whole chapter called 'Don't Forget Your Neighbors' on finding compatibility with the boy next door. Actually, that's the chapter that gave me the idea to go looking in the Drama Department. They're my neighbors at the university."

Phoebe stretched her legs out, propping them on Elise's coffee table. "Let's have it. What does Ms. Jasmine advise?"

"'Sometimes the way to a man's heart *is* through his stomach,'" Elise read. "'Bake him a batch of welcome-to-the-neighborhood brownies.'"

"Would you believe Frannie already tried that? He's allergic to chocolate."

"Hmm. Oh, how about this one? 'Is the man an animal lover? You could accidentally-on-purpose lose your dog or cat in his yard—'"

"Been there, done that. He had no interest in rescuing Daisy's cat from a tree."

"Darn, he *is* a tough case." Elise flipped the page, scanning the text for gems. "Here's one—'Next time you have a domestic emergency, before you call a plumber or electrician, try the boy next door. If you're lucky, he'll be anxious to show off his manly prowess with power tools. Even if the two of you don't hit it off, you could save yourself an exorbitant repair bill.'"

"Are you forgetting about Bill?" Phoebe said. Bill White was the super at Mesa Blue. He kept the building in top shape.

"You're right. No one would impose on a neighbor when Bill is around. Okay, one more idea. 'Have a party and invite him. If he comes alone, good for you. If he comes with a date, be gracious to them both. They might have eligible male friends. If he doesn't come, you can always make so much noise that he can't resist coming over to join the fun.'"

"That's it!" Phoebe cried. "Why didn't I think of that?"

"I thought you hated parties," Elise said. "You said you'd had enough of them in L.A. to last you a lifetime."

Phoebe wrinkled her nose at the reminder. Those Hollywood parties had seemed exciting when she'd first moved to California. She'd loved the schmoozing—name-brand producers making promises, aging movie stars making passes, other agents trying to steal her away from the one she already had. And all of them telling her how beautiful she was.

About the time she'd landed the part as Vanessa Vance on the nighttime soap opera "Skin Deep," however, the schmoozing got old. Everyone assumed she'd slept with the handsome producer just to get the part.

People would have laughed if she'd told them the real reason she'd gotten involved with Joel Spinner. She'd thought she was in love with him. She hadn't realized what a can of worms she'd opened. Joel had been less than discreet about their affair, and next thing she knew, the studly young star of the show assumed she would sleep with *him*. And when she didn't, he told everybody she had.

For a few weeks, she was labeled Hollywood's slut-*du-jour*. Unfortunately, she couldn't claim complete innocence. On the rebound from Joel, she'd made a few bad choices in the romance department.

Still, she never sank to the level of sleeping with someone just to get a part, though the opportunities were there. And once it became obvious Phoebe Lane didn't play the casting-couch game, she went from rising young star to has-been in a short time span. Vanessa Vance was killed in an unsightly car wreck. The soap got canned. And her agent expected her to do the next round of parties—only this time it would be harder, because she was no longer the freshest face in town.

And she had a bit of a rep.

That's when she'd made her escape from Hollywood, much to her mother's disappointment.

"My party would be nothing like those parties in L.A.," Phoebe said. "Anyway, I don't know why I didn't think of this before. As one of your best friends, I *must* give you and James an engagement party."

"Oh, but I wasn't hinting around," Elise objected.

"I know. But it's a great idea, anyway. Start making out your guest list. Your family—that'll be a crowd right there—James's family, and all our neighbors. We'll have it out by the pool!"

Mesa Blue was a horseshoe-shaped building situated around a huge, blue-bottomed pool, which was another reason Phoebe had jumped at the chance to move here. Phoebe loved to swim. These days, while doing her laps, she worked out chemical equations from her organic chemistry class in her mind. The pool area was perfect for gatherings large and small, and anybody who lived here was free to make use of it.

"You know, this isn't a bad idea," Elise said. "I bet you can get Jeff to tend bar for you." Jeff Hawkin was the kid who maintained the pool and courtyard grounds. He also was a part-time bartender at The Prickly Pear, a nearby bar and grill that Phoebe, Elise and Daisy had made their home-away-from-home.

"Great idea. Maybe I can get The Prickly Pear to cater it."

Soon, Phoebe and Elise were hip-deep in party plans. The invitation list included a few bonus eligible men for Daisy, per Jane Jasmine's advice: "Hedge your bets," Jane had written. "You can invite any number of single men to a party, and none will know he's being 'singled out' for attention."

WHEN WYATT OPENED the colorful envelope that had been slipped under his door, he suspected ulterior motives. The flowing, feminine script was a clue. Sure, it was just an invitation to a party to celebrate the engagement of one of his neighbors, Elise Foster. His grandparents had mentioned her, too—many times. But the personal note from the party's hostess, none other than Phoebe Lane, confirmed his suspicions.

"Everyone would really like to get to know you," she'd written. "Hope you'll be able to make it."

He had to admit he was tempted. Though his co-workers at the studio had invited him time and again to socialize with them after their day's work, he always declined. He simply had too much to do. Eventually he would delegate more responsibilities, as he collected a loyal and competent staff. But right now he felt compelled to oversee every detail personally. Interviewing potential guests took hours out of every day, but he insisted that all people to appear on the show be thoroughly screened. The last thing he wanted was for "Heads Up" to turn into another daytime trash TV show.

His grandparents would have urged him to go to the party. They'd told him often enough how much fun it was to live at Mesa Blue because of the nice neighbors. They'd made lifelong friends here.

So Phoebe's invitation was tempting. Wyatt would have liked to meet new friends, people he could relax with—let down his guard, talk about anything and everything. A woman friend would be nice, too. He'd been without serious female companionship for longer than was healthy. But a party wasn't the place for him to meet friends of either sex. In his experience, parties were where publicity-hungry people of every ilk tried every persuasive trick they could think of to to get themselves on TV.

It had been bad enough in Chicago, where he'd produced a local morning talk show. But since "Heads Up" had made its moderately successful debut, closet wanna-be celebrities were coming out of the woodwork.

Griffin, one of the security guards downstairs, had started singing "Moon River" one night as Wyatt had entered the building from work, dead tired. A housekeeper who cleaned his office at work had left a folder on his desk filled with nude pictures. It just got worse and worse.

If everybody in the building didn't already know about his job, he might have considered attending the party. But he knew his grandparents well enough to know they'd bragged about him to anybody who would listen. They'd raised him after his parents' sudden death, and for some odd reason they thought he was perfect.

That settled it, Wyatt thought. Then he dropped the pretty invitation in his kitchen trash, but not without a sigh of regret.

Chapter Two

Phoebe was pleased with how quickly she'd pulled together Elise and James's engagement party. The Prickly Pear was setting up a *fajita* buffet in the courtyard; Jeff had agreed to tend bar, though Phoebe suspected what he really wanted was to keep an eye on his precious pool, the maintenance of which he took very seriously. Invitations had gone out and RSVPs had come back. Almost all Elise's siblings were coming—she had seven—along with some of James's family and even his housekeeper, whom Phoebe gathered was more like a family member than an employee.

Phoebe had gotten some personalized cocktail napkins printed. She and Daisy had pitched in on a gift of his-and-her massages, even though Elise had made them promise no gifts. The weather was cooperating—it was a balmy 74 degrees.

Now all Phoebe had to do was get herself ready, and that was the easy part. As a former model and actress, she could do hair, clothes and makeup in nothing flat. Because she'd had time to spare, she'd applied an avocado, honey and yogurt facial mask—

her own invention, very popular at the Sunrise Spa where she worked doing beauty makeovers.

Now she sat in her living room in a beanbag chair, studying her organic chemistry book. She was a bit behind on her studying because of the extra time planning the party had taken, and she had a test on Monday—but she would have all day tomorrow to study. She'd specifically requested Sunday off, though her boss hadn't liked it.

After a few minutes of letting the mask do its thing, Phoebe consulted her watch. It was about time to jump in the shower. She stood and reached for the hem of her slip, intending to pull it off gingerly over her head so as not to get avocado all over it, then heard a noise—a *horrible* noise that sounded like nothing so much as Niagara Falls. And it was coming from her utility room.

She ran through the kitchen, then skidded to a stop at the entrance to the small room where she did her laundry. It was, indeed, a waterfall, or maybe a geyser, pouring noisily from behind her washing machine. Water gushed everywhere!

"Oh, my gosh, oh, my gosh." Phoebe stepped back into the kitchen and dialed Bill White's number, which was posted with her other emergency numbers. Bill's voice came on the line.

"Bill, Bill! Come quick, my—"

"I'm not in right now," Bill's recorded voice informed her. *"Please leave your name and number—"*

Phoebe hung up. No time, no time. If she waited for Bill to return from wherever, her entire apartment would be flooded and the water would be leaking downstairs into Elise's apartment. She started to dial 911. This was an emergency, right? No—the police wouldn't come for a leak.

Phoebe was almost paralyzed by her quandary. Then she saw water running from the utility room onto the tiled kitchen floor. The living room carpets were next.

Who in the building could she— Wyatt! Of course. Hadn't he been working on the sink the one and only time she'd seen him? Without further debate, she ran for the front door, out into the hallway and around the corner. She banged on Wyatt's door with her fist.

"Wyatt! Help, please, I need you!"

NOW THERE WAS SOMETHING a man didn't hear every day, Wyatt thought as he laid down his calculator, distracted from his weekly "Heads Up" budget fiasco by a seductive female voice calling for help. Calling his name. Claiming to *need* him.

Yeah, right, he thought. When he opened the front door, some winsome female would be waiting for him—and what kind of story would she have? Maybe a big bug in her kitchen, or a jar that needed opening...or something in her eye?

He almost ignored the summons. He'd lived in Mesa Blue for nearly two weeks and had so far managed to stay handily out of his neighbors' way. But when the woman called again for help, he realized she did sound a little hysterical. What if something was really wrong? His grandparents would never forgive him if he let some harm befall Phoebe Lane.

That was who the voice belonged to, he realized.

Though he'd only heard it once, he remembered it, smooth as warm honey. Even when hysterical.

He hurried to the door and opened it. The creature standing in the hallway was hardly a female trying to impress him. Oh, the costume could have been contrived. After all, a woman dressed only in a slip could certainly catch a man's attention. Especially *this* woman, for she had a better-than-average body, tall and slim-hipped, with full breasts and legs up to... But above the neck, she reminded him of the Creature from the Black Lagoon, wearing some kind of pea-green goo all over her face.

Wyatt would have laughed, but she didn't give him the chance. She grabbed his arm and dragged him toward her apartment.

"You fix plumbing, right?" she asked breathlessly. "I saw you under the sink. You know pipes, water?"

"Uh, some, yeah."

She pushed through her front door. Immediately Wyatt heard the water running. "In there." She pointed toward her kitchen, where a lake of water was spilling onto the living room carpet.

"Oh, hell." He ran for the kitchen, splashed through it and into the utility room, where the problem became glaringly apparent. Her washing machine hose had burst. He took a deep breath and plunged into the gushing spray of water, groping around behind the washing machine, feeling his way until he found the shut-off valve. A couple of turns, and the geyser shrank away to nothing.

"Oh, oh, thank heavens. I didn't know what to do, and Bill wasn't in—"

"Do you have buckets?"

"Buckets?" She blinked at him with huge blue eyes. Those eyes, surrounded as they were by green glop, made her look like a frog.

"And mops. We better get this water cleaned up before it soaks into the subfloor. Or, worse yet, into your downstairs neighbor's ceiling."

Phoebe gasped, then immediately went to work locating what he'd asked for. "Elise would kill me. She's trying to sell her unit."

"Oh. She's the one getting married." He took a bucket from her and started scooping up water from the floor, then dumping it into the sink. Phoebe got a mop and pitched in herself.

Wyatt gave Elise's condo more than a passing thought. Though he'd been looking for a house to live in ever since he'd moved to Phoenix, it might not be that bad living in a condo, especially one as nice as those in Mesa Blue. Plus, if he lived here, he would be close to his grandparents. They were in good health now, still traveling and running around like a couple of kids. But they were both in their eighties. He wanted to keep an eye on them.

"Do you know how much she's asking?" Wyatt asked idly, his gaze focused on Phoebe's shapely backside, as she vigorously mopped the floor. He was a bun man, he couldn't deny it, and Phoebe's was tautly muscled and slender, but womanly all at the same time. And what exactly was she wearing under that slip? A thong, or...nothing?

His mouth suddenly dry, he looked purposefully away from her, grateful that he was soaked with cold water. He had no business ogling a woman in a slip, especially a woman who was so rattled by nearly flooding her entire apartment that she'd forgotten she wasn't decently dressed.

He silently apologized for believing she'd orchestrated such a disaster solely to get his attention.

"I'm not sure how much she's asking," Phoebe said. "But you can ask her tonight at the party. I know your grandparents would be tickled to have you move in here. Gosh, I just realized I haven't even introduced myself. I'm Phoebe Lane."

"The one with the wayward kitten," Wyatt said, as if he'd only just now made the connection.

"Actually, that was Frannie's kitten. I was just trying to help."

The worst of the water was up now. "It's nice to meet you, Phoebe." Wyatt held out his hand. She shook it quickly, then let go. Her hand was soft, yet strong, her fingernails long, tapered, and painted a pale peach. He noticed her hair, then, too. Though it was pulled back with a rubber band, he could see that it was long, almost to her waist, and straight as a waterfall.

"I can finish up here," she said. "I guess you might like some time to get ready for the party yourself."

Wyatt rubbed his unshaved chin. Perhaps he shouldn't have been so quick to criticize Phoebe's appearance; he was hardly a fashion plate himself. At least he'd showered this morning, but he'd thrown on the first clothes he found: an old, holey pair of jeans and a T-shirt with a cable station logo.

"Oh, I won't be at the party tonight," he said, the regret in his voice almost genuine. He was curious to see what this Phoebe looked like when she slicked herself up.

Phoebe's green face fell. "I'm sorry to hear that. Everybody is…well, that is, your grandparents have told us so much about you, but we haven't had a chance to get to know you."

"I've been busy. And I have paperwork to finish tonight."

"You work in television or something, right?"

This was uneasy territory. "Yeah, at WBZZ," he murmured, hoping she'd assume he was a lighting technician. But chances were his grandparents had told her everything.

Surprisingly, she didn't pursue that line of questioning.

"You still have to eat dinner. Just drop by for a few minutes and grab some *fajitas*. You don't have to dress up or anything, it's very casual."

"I don't think—"

"Please say yes. There are so many nice people living at Mesa Blue. Like Daisy Redford, for example."

"Who?"

"Daisy Redford. She's the most incredible artist. The most gorgeous auburn hair. I'm surprised your grandparents never mentioned her. They have her over for dinner all the time."

They *had* mentioned her. Numerous times, almost as often as they mentioned Phoebe. But it seemed his grandparents weren't the only ones interested in playing matchmaker. Phoebe was being none too subtle. Did her trying to push Daisy on him mean she wasn't interested herself?

And why should he care whether frog-woman found him attractive?

"I appreciate the invitation, really, but I just don't have time to socialize. My work takes up all of my time."

Her manner turned definitely cool. "I'd better let you get back to it, then. Thanks again for stopping the leak."

"No problem. I just hope you can get that stuff off your face after all this time."

"What?" She reached up and touched her face. Her eyes, already huge, grew to the size of saucers.

He didn't wait around for the inevitable shrieks of consternation, preferring to make a hasty escape.

PHOEBE RAN to the bathroom and looked at herself in the mirror. It was worse than she had imagined. Not only had she forgotten about the avocado-honey-yogurt mask, but she'd also been running around in nothing but her slip! She'd just been so panicked by the flood that she'd forgotten herself completely. Then, when she'd seen Wyatt Madison, she'd gone totally brainless.

His buns had made her mouth go dry the other day, but the rest of him measured up just fine—broad shoulders, nice pecs, washboard stomach, all revealed in unbearable detail because his T-shirt had gotten soaking wet. His face wouldn't stop a clock, either, featuring chiseled, matinee-idol features, intriguingly dark gray eyes, even white teeth. Lots of the guys she'd worked with in television would envy that face, which she was certain no plastic surgeon or cosmetic dentist had gone near. He was a hundred-percent authentic. She was amazed he'd chosen to stay behind the camera.

Even after she'd showered, dressed and put on makeup, Phoebe couldn't get Wyatt Madison off her mind. He was older than she'd expected, probably closer to forty than thirty. The most recent picture displayed by the Madisons was Wyatt's high school graduation picture. Though Phoebe realized he wouldn't still look as he had in high school—which was cute, with a killer smile—she hadn't realized he was so mature. He even had a bit of gray at his temples. The Madisons had made him sound more like a carefree playboy than a stodgy TV executive.

Well, okay, he wasn't stodgy. He was gorgeous. And Daisy was looking for someone mature, ready to settle down, right? So Phoebe had dutifully mentioned her to Wyatt. But she'd had to force herself, as a traitorous little part of her psyche wanted to keep him to herself.

"Hah, fat chance," she said to her image. She inspired some degree of lust in most men she met. That just came with the territory when a woman had the good fortune, as Phoebe did, to be born with Nordic genes that came through loud and clear. But in Wyatt, she'd probably inspired nothing but disgust, running around in a slip and a lumpy green face.

Which was good, she decided. She didn't want or need a man in her life, especially not a man involved in the entertainment industry. She'd had her fill of all those phony smooth talkers with their cell phones and their bottled water and their five-hundred-dollar sunglasses. It seemed like every guy she'd met in L.A. with even a tiny connection to movies or television had tried to parlay his perceived power into an invitation to bed.

The faint strains of accordion drifting into her apartment reminded her that the party was getting started without her—and she was the hostess! With one last pat to her hair, she headed down to the courtyard.

Daisy was watching for her, and ran up the moment Phoebe appeared. "Where have you been?"

"Had a plumbing emergency, almost a disaster. Everything looks great!" She had to raise her voice to be heard over the *mariachi* music. Hiring the quartet had seemed like a good idea at the time, but she hadn't realized the music would be so loud. Fortunately, just about everybody in the whole building was at the party, so the music volume shouldn't bother anyone.

Except maybe Wyatt Madison, the old curmudgeon.

"You've got to see Elise's dress," Daisy said. "She looks so great! Ever since you did that makeover for her, she's seemed so, oh, I don't know, glamorous."

"She wasn't exactly chopped liver *before* the makeover," Phoebe said, pausing to shake hands with the real estate agent who lived in 3A, on the other side of the Madisons.

"When are you going to do a makeover for me?" Daisy asked. "After all, I'm the one trying to attract a husband." All Phoebe could do was laugh. Daisy, with her chin-length auburn hair and flashing green eyes, had the kind of striking personal style Phoebe wouldn't dare tamper with. Tonight she wore a green, batik gauze dress—probably designed and hand-dyed by her clothing-designer mother—and chunky jade jewelry that set off her delicate good looks to perfection. She ran a trendy art gallery, Native Art, and she was a wonderfully gifted potter herself, though she was far too modest about her talent.

Men ought to be standing in line to marry her, Phoebe thought, but so far her and Elise's attempts to find Daisy a suitable mate had met with dismal failure—despite the best of advice from author Jane Jasmine.

"There ought to be some good candidates here tonight," Phoebe said, grabbing a tortilla chip off the buffet table as they passed. "With all of Elise's siblings coming—"

"They're all girls. Except one, but I don't think he'll be here."

"Oh, right, the oldest one, the lawyer. What's his name?"

"I forget," Daisy said airily. "I didn't meet him that time he came over to Elise's, remember? I was hiding in her bedroom with curlers and green stuff all over my face."

At the mention of the green mask, all Phoebe could think about was her own earlier humiliation.

"Hey, what about Wyatt Madison?" Daisy asked, as if she'd just read Phoebe's mind. "Isn't he supposed to be here?"

Phoebe's heart fluttered for half a second, then calmed. "Oh, I meant to tell you. He's not coming."

"Darn," Daisy said, though she sounded as if she really didn't care much. "I'm dying to know what he's like. He couldn't possibly be the paragon his grandparents make him out to be.''

"He's not,'' Phoebe said.

Daisy's delicate eyebrows arched. "Oh, really? Do tell—you're holding out, girlfriend.''

"I just met him tonight. He's *old.*''

"Old?'' Daisy looked puzzled. "How old could he be? He has grandparents.''

"He's at least…thirty-eight. And he's got gray hair.''

"Really? I like gray hair. Well, I mean, on some men it looks distinguished.''

Phoebe wouldn't have used the word *distinguished* to describe Wyatt. His grandfather Rolland, maybe. Wyatt would probably look like Rolland someday. But currently, he was more dangerous-looking than distinguished.

"So what happened? How'd you meet him?''

Phoebe quickly told Daisy the horror story.

Daisy laughed until tears rolled down her pink cheeks. "That green mask is cursed! Well, at least I don't have to worry about competition from you! He's probably written you right off his list as Avocado Woman with Plumbing Problems.''

Phoebe was afraid Daisy was right. "As if. I'm not looking, you know.''

"Like that matters. Every guy you meet falls all over you. I mean, what guy doesn't fantasize about dating a movie star?''

"One lousy part in a really bad soap opera doesn't make me a movie star,'' Phoebe said. "Oh, there's Bill. I have to tell him about my washer hose.''

"I'm heading for the margarita machine. You want one?"

Phoebe nodded. After her plumbing ordeal, she could use a dozen, but she'd settle for one.

"Well, hey there, Phoebe," Bill White said. He sat at a small table, working on a plate full of *fajitas*. "You're looking beautiful, as always."

"Thank you," Phoebe said automatically. "Where were you an hour ago? I was in desperate need."

Bill shot a quick, guilty look toward Frannie, who sat at the same table but pretended not to pay attention to him. "Oh, just around. What's the problem?"

"I'll tell you about it tomorrow," Phoebe said, realizing that Bill, who had *always* been available to fix any problem, had probably for once in his life turned off his beeper because he'd been spending time with Frannie. Bill and Frannie had been making cow eyes at each other for years, both of them too shy to do anything about their mutual crush. But Elise had set them up on a date a few weeks ago, and despite a shaky start, now they were something of an item.

Cupid had been busy, Phoebe mused as she left them to find Elise and James. Now, if only he'd shoot Daisy with one of his little arrows.

Phoebe spent the next few minutes meeting some of James's friends and family, including his jovial housekeeper, MaryBelle, whom he clearly adored like a favorite aunt.

"You look so familiar," MaryBelle had said at once. "Wait, I, oh, I know! Vanessa Vance! You look exactly like that woman on 'Skin Deep'!"

"That was me," Phoebe admitted. By now she was used to being recognized, though it happened less and less often as "Skin Deep" faded from the public memory.

At least MaryBelle didn't gush. "I was really mad when they killed off Vanessa," she said quietly. "You were the best one on the show. It got canceled right after you left."

Phoebe smiled, no longer bitter about the experience.

"Why didn't you get on another show?" Mary-Belle asked innocently. "Or in the movies? You were good enough."

"I tried," Phoebe said. She'd gone on lots of auditions, but she never got cast in anything except bit parts and a vacuum cleaner commercial. "I guess my heart just wasn't in it anymore. I'm glad to be out of Hollywood."

MaryBelle gave her a sympathetic pat on the hand, then went on to chat with one of Elise's sisters. Elise herself slipped away from the knot of her family and joined Phoebe, who was straightening a stack of napkins and putting out more forks on the buffet table.

"You look thirsty," Elise commented.

"Daisy was going to bring me something, but she's disappeared."

"Come on, I'll walk over to the bar with you," Elise said. Then she whispered, "Any sign of Mr. Mysterious yet?"

Phoebe repeated her appalling tale yet again, as they ambled toward the far side of the courtyard where the bar had been set up.

"So he's not coming?" Elise asked, disappointed. "How are we ever going to set him up with Daisy if he hides in his apartment like a hibernating bear?"

"You know, I just don't think he's right for Daisy," Phoebe found herself saying. "He's a workaholic. And he's too old."

"Too old?" Elise repeated.

"At least thirty-eight."

Elise laughed. "So? Daisy's thirty. What's the big deal?"

Phoebe shrugged. "I don't know."

"Trying to keep him for yourself, huh?" Elise teased.

"No!" Phoebe's denial was quick and emphatic.

Elise looked at her curiously.

"You *know* I'm much too busy to even look at a man, but if I wasn't, which I am, I certainly wouldn't look at him. He works in television, and you know how I can't stand to be around—"

Phoebe halted her tirade. Elise was grinning at her.

WYATT RAN DOWN the column of numbers one more time, tapping them into his calculator, but he got yet a third different total. How could he possibly concentrate with that damn *mariachi* music blaring from the courtyard?

He certainly hoped these weekend parties weren't a regular event at Mesa Blue. How could his grandparents stand it?

Hell, he knew the answer to that question. If they weren't on vacation, they'd be down in the thick of the party, probably starting a conga line. But his grandparents didn't have to show up at a meeting Monday morning with a revised budget for "Heads Up."

It wasn't just the music that bugged him. It was the

chatter. The laughter. All those people yukking it up. Half of them probably didn't even know Elise and What's-His-Name, they just came for the free food and free drinks.

Wyatt tried one more time to focus on his addition, but it was no use. The band's lead singer was now doing a very bad Julio Iglesias impression. Someone had to put a stop to this.

He set down his ledger and calculator, slid into some loafers and started for his front door. He could have simply yelled off his balcony for the party-goers to keep it down, but that seemed a little déclassé, and his grandparents wouldn't be pleased if he antagonized all their neighbors.

He would find Phoebe and discreetly request that either her so-called musicians put a sock in it, or he'd call the cops.

As he reached for the front doorknob, he looked down at himself. The jeans and T-shirt he'd exchanged for the ones he'd gotten wet at Phoebe's were pretty disreputable. He toyed with the idea of changing—just so he wouldn't call attention to himself—but he finally decided against it. He wasn't planning on staying long enough for anyone to form an opinion about him.

When he stepped into the courtyard, the guests were so thick he could have stirred them with a stick. How would he ever find Phoebe in this mess? Then it occurred to him that he wouldn't recognize Phoebe, anyway, unless she happened to be wearing guacamole from the buffet.

He searched the crowd, his gaze finally stopping on a pretty lady with dark red hair sitting alone at the end of the pool, her bare feet dangling in the water as she nursed a frothy drink.

She happened to look up just then, catching him watching her, and she smiled warmly. Since no one else paid the slightest attention to him, Wyatt decided to ask the woman to help him find Phoebe. He walked determinedly over to her.

"You're Wyatt, right?" she said, before he could get a word out. "Have a seat." She patted the concrete beside her.

He hadn't intended to spend any time at the party. But the redhead looked lonely, so he joined her. "How'd you know who I am?" he asked.

"You look just like your grandfather. Well, like he probably did forty years ago. He's a handsome man."

"Thank you."

"Oh, I didn't mean…" She blushed prettily. "You probably think I'm flirting with you now."

"Would that be so terrible?"

"No. I mean, yes, because I don't usually flirt. Phoebe sent you over here, didn't she?" the woman said miserably.

"Actually, your smile brought me over here."

"Now who's flirting?"

Maybe he was. Maybe that was because the redhead put him completely at ease. Though she was undeniably pretty, with that gorgeous auburn hair, he could tell right away there wasn't a bit of chemistry between them. If they got to know each other at all, it would be as friends.

"I'm Daisy Redford. Phoebe said you weren't coming."

Daisy Redford! Alarm bells went off in Wyatt's

head. This was the one Phoebe had been praising earlier.

"Is Phoebe trying to set us up?" Wyatt asked point-blank.

Daisy's eyes grew huge. She tried to sputter a denial, but she wasn't a good liar. Finally she said in a small voice, "They just wanted me to meet you, Phoebe and Elise, that is."

"Why?"

Daisy shrugged, looking supremely uncomfortable. "Why not?" Then she laughed. "It was a dumb idea. Setups hardly ever work. Phoebe set me up with this dentist... My friends are not going to be happy I foiled all their plans for you and me."

"You don't look like the kind of girl who needs a setup," Wyatt said. "And that's an honest observation. I'm not flirting."

"Nice of you to say. So what made you decide to show up after you told Phoebe you couldn't come?" Daisy asked, not sounding quite so shy. Apparently he'd put her at ease, too, now that they'd set aside any romantic potential between them.

"I was going to complain about the noise," Wyatt admitted.

"The band is kind of loud," Daisy agreed. "I'll come with you to talk to Phoebe, if you want." She started to pull her feet out of the pool, but Wyatt stopped her.

"No, no, that's not necessary. I've changed my mind. I won't get any more work done tonight, and I'm here now, so I might as well enjoy myself. Where is our hostess, anyway?"

But he saw her then—with that fall of straight

blond hair, she was impossible to miss. She stood near the bar with another woman, laughing with the bartender, whom Wyatt recognized as the guy who took care of Mesa Blue's pool.

Without a green face, she was the most enchanting creature he'd ever seen. Not at all frog-like.

"I guess you spotted her," Daisy said, giving him a knowing look.

Chapter Three

Wyatt closed his mouth. He'd been gaping at Phoebe like a lovesick schoolboy worshipping the head cheerleader from afar.

"She's pretty hard to miss," Daisy said. "I can't understand why she didn't get snapped up to star in some blockbuster movie when she was in Hollywood."

"She's an *actress?*" Wyatt asked, horrified. Somehow, his grandparents had neglected to tell him that part.

"Oh, yeah, don't you recognize her? Vanessa Vance. From 'Skin Deep.'" When Wyatt made no acknowledgment, she added, "You know, that nighttime soap a few years ago?"

"I, um, don't usually watch soaps."

"You didn't miss much. The show was horrible. The only thing good about it was Phoebe. Then they went and killed off her character, the ratings tanked, and it got canceled."

"She's an actress," he repeated. He could almost feel a wall going up around him. Lord save him from wanna-be movie stars and has-been starlets.

Phoebe *had* to know what he did for a living. His grandparents would have told her. So why wasn't she all over him, trying to get on TV? A little national exposure on "Heads Up" could revive a stalled acting career.

"She's not acting now," Daisy said. "She's st—" Daisy abruptly stopped. "She does beauty makeovers at the Sunrise Spa. But if you ask me, her talents are wasted there. She's a lot smarter than that."

The words *actress* and *smart* did not belong in the same discussion, Wyatt mused. Maybe Phoebe hadn't hit him up yet. But she would. He could only surmise that she had some more elaborate scheme for getting to him. Something that would work better than throwing cat food onto his balcony.

STANDING NEAR the bar chatting with Elise, Phoebe savored the last few drops of her frozen margarita. She wanted another one because it was a warm evening, but she had a lot of studying to do tomorrow and couldn't afford to wake up even slightly hungover. Since she seldom drank alcohol, it wouldn't take much to give her a fuzzy head in the morning.

"Can I have a cola, Jeff, please?" she asked.

Jeff winked. "Sure thing, gorgeous. What'll you give me in return?"

Phoebe snorted. Jeff was all of twenty-two and an inveterate flirt. But he was harmless. She suspected if she ever responded to his blatant come-ons, he'd run for the hills.

"I guess I better get back to my hostessly duties," she said to Elise, as Jeff handed her the cola.

"And I better find my fiancé. I worked hard enough to get him. It'd be a shame to lose him now."

They were about to turn and head for their various destinations when a man came up behind Elise and put his hands over her eyes. "Guess who?"

It took Phoebe a moment to realize this was Chance, Elise's brother. He'd called earlier in the week to say he couldn't come.

"Chance! What are you doing here?" Elise turned and hugged her brother. He looked especially handsome tonight, Phoebe thought, in casual khakis and a pale green knit shirt. She adored a man who dressed well. He put Wyatt and his old T-shirt to shame.

Then why was it her thoughts turned so frequently to how that T-shirt had molded to the planes of Wyatt's chest, and the way his faded jeans had hugged his butt?

"My meeting got canceled," Chance said. "Hi, Phoebe. I hope it's okay that I showed up without warning."

"No problem."

"Hey, Elise," he said, voice lowered, "who's that gorgeous woman sitting with her feet in the pool?"

Elise looked in the direction Chance indicated, but she saw no one. "Who?"

Chance blinked a couple of times, as if his eyes were playing tricks on him. "She was there a minute ago. If I find her, will you introduce us?"

Elise gave him a playful tap on the arm. "You are not allowed to hit on any woman who's a friend of mine. You'll just break her heart, and then she'll blame it on me."

"Okay, okay! Jeez."

Chance rubbed his arm, though Phoebe suspected Elise couldn't possibly do him any damage, even if she tried. He had pretty good muscles for a lawyer.

"I'll make my own introductions." With a mischievous smile, he sauntered off, apparently intent on finding the object of his lust.

Elise rolled her eyes. "He's hopeless."

"But he's cute. Why don't we introduce him to Daisy?" Phoebe suggested.

Elise shook her head. "He is definitely not father material. Anyway, looks like Daisy's otherwise occupied." She nodded toward the buffet table. "Phoebe, who's that she's talking to?"

Phoebe peered at her friend, so easy to spot with that auburn hair shining in the light of the torches they'd set up for the party. Daisy was engaged in cozy conversation with a man. And not just any man.

"Holy cow, that's Wyatt Madison."

"You're kidding," Elise said. "I thought he wasn't coming."

"He said he wasn't. What's he doing here?"

"Enjoying himself, it looks like," Elise said. "And look at Daisy. She's laughing."

"Holy cow."

"What's wrong with you?" Elise said. "This is exactly what we wanted! Maybe he's the perfect one for Daisy."

"He's too old for her," Phoebe said. "Now that I see them together, they just don't look good. You know, as a couple."

"Phoebe!" Elise objected.

"Maybe we shouldn't have thrust them together," Phoebe went on. "What if—"

"We didn't 'thrust them together.' They found each other. Chill, Phoebes."

"I think Chance would be a better bet. He's gorgeous, nice, gainfully employed—"

"Don't even start. I love Chance with all my heart, but he's a cad in the worst sense of the word. Daisy's looking for a husband, remember? A potential father for her potential baby. The last thing she needs is a guy who thinks *wife* is a four-letter word."

"It is a four-letter word."

"You know what I mean."

"Well, I still think he'd be better than Wyatt Mad—" Phoebe stopped mid-name, then blinked her eyes a couple of times to clear them. Surely after one margarita she couldn't be hallucinating.

"What's wrong?" Elise asked.

"Daisy and Wyatt. They're gone." The buffet table, where they'd been huddling a few moments earlier, was now empty.

"Hmm. They certainly are. Maybe they hit it off, and they've gone somewhere a bit more private."

"Bite your tongue."

"Phoebe!"

"What do we really know about Wyatt Madison? What his grandparents have told us, and they're partial. He's in the entertainment industry, and that's a strike against him. You have no idea what kind of wolves work in television. He could be an ax murderer!"

Elise just gave her a long-suffering look. "I was just kidding before when I suggested you wanted to keep Wyatt for yourself. But you keep this up, I'll start to believe you really do want him."

"Oh, don't be ridiculous. Besides, that would be almost incestuous. The Madisons think of me as their daughter, and they raised Wyatt as their own son—"

"You're making excuses."

Phoebe would have argued more, but Elise's fiancé, James Dillon, approached them. Or rather, he approached Elise. Phoebe doubted he even saw her there. He was so completely in love with Elise, he only had eyes for her.

"I've been looking all over for you," he chastised gently, kissing her on the cheek.

Phoebe quietly sighed. Watching Elise and James fall in love had been fun. Elise had never been so happy. James was absolute proof that good men did exist. Still, in Phoebe's experience, they were few and far between.

Phoebe's mother had always told her she had everything she needed to land herself a good husband— drop-dead good looks and a body that wouldn't quit. Phoebe hadn't found her mother's advice to be true. After the Hollywood fiasco, she had stopped thinking about husbands, and men in general. She was creating her own future, one in which she wouldn't have to depend on her sex appeal to bring her success. Nor would she have to depend on another person—husband, boss, casting director, agent, plastic surgeon, whoever.

"You are way too gorgeous to be standing around by yourself," Jeff said. "Wanta blow this joint and go make our own action?"

Phoebe smiled. "You have to work and I'm the hostess. I can't disappear. Otherwise, I'd jump at such an attractive invitation."

Jeff shrugged. "Can't blame a guy for trying."

PHOEBE AWOKE the next morning feeling unsettled and not very well rested. Then she realized why. Daisy and Wyatt had disappeared last night, and she hadn't seen either of them for the rest of the evening.

Daisy was very vulnerable. Recently her doctor had told her that if she ever wanted to have children, she needed to do it now, before her endometriosis rendered her infertile. Daisy *did* want children, very much. But she refused to have a baby without a husband. She'd been a "love child" herself, and no kid of hers was growing up without a father.

Now Daisy was so focused on the idea of finding Mr. Right and settling down that her usually keen powers of discernment might be impaired. If Wyatt had taken advantage of Daisy's clouded judgment, Phoebe would string him up by his toes!

Phoebe hopped in the shower to clear the fuzz from her mind, threw on a pair of overalls and a purple ribbed shirt, then grabbed the phone and dialed Daisy's number.

No answer. Even the answering machine didn't pick up. That was a bad sign.

Phoebe went out into the hallway and walked slowly past Wyatt's door. His newspaper was out in the hallway, uncollected. Another bad sign.

She stopped right in front of the door. Then she pressed her ear against it. Nothing, darn it. Then again, the walls and doors at Mesa Blue were extraordinarily well insulated.

Just then the door jerked open, and Phoebe pitched

forward. A strong pair of arms prevented her from falling flat on her face.

"Good morning to you, too," Wyatt said, setting her back on her feet.

"Oh, uh…" *Think, Phoebe!* And she'd better come up with an excuse real fast. But somehow, she couldn't think of anything but those strong arms catching her.

Wyatt bent down and retrieved the paper. He wore only a pair of running shorts—no shirt, no shoes.

"I came to borrow some, um, coffee," Phoebe finally said. "I'm all out, and I really need the caffeine."

He smiled as if he didn't believe her for an instant. "I don't drink coffee, and my grandparents don't have any, either."

Phoebe tried to nonchalantly peer past him into the apartment for any sign of Daisy. But Wyatt seemed intent on blocking her view with his annoyingly well-muscled chest, making it hard to look at anything else.

"I have orange juice," he offered.

"No, thanks. Sorry to bother you."

Phoebe fled. She didn't know what else to do in the face of all that overwhelming maleness. She didn't look back, she just scurried into her own apartment and slammed the door.

Damn! What an awful time for her hormones to act up. Living in L.A., after a few of those will-you-respect-me-in-the-morning liaisons, she'd gotten disgusted with herself and made it a blanket policy to just say no. She'd virtually shut down her sexual responses to men.

It had been years since she'd even thought about getting involved with a man, and she liked it that way. Her track record was abysmal when it came to romance, anyway. The few relationships she'd ventured into had never progressed past shallow and physical. Men she'd dated had just never wanted to know anything about her except her erogenous zones.

Now, when she least needed it, her body had reawakened. To Wyatt Madison, of all people. Was Elise right? Had she been against Daisy and Wyatt getting together because she wanted to save Wyatt for herself?

No, she told herself firmly. Maybe Wyatt wasn't an ax murderer, and maybe he had nice grandparents, but that didn't mean he could seduce Daisy on their first meeting and get away with it. Phoebe had to find out what really happened last night and be prepared for damage control with Daisy.

Fortified with new resolve and a new plan, she headed down to Frannie's apartment. She would spy on Wyatt's balcony from Frannie's patio. There was a good chance that if he had an overnight guest, the two of them would sit out on the balcony to read the paper, drink their orange juice, and enjoy the marvelous spring weather amongst Helen's potted forest of green.

But Frannie wasn't home, either. Was she with Bill, maybe?

Phoebe was not to be dissuaded. She marched back up to the third floor, and after hesitating only a moment to ask herself, *Are you crazy?* she knocked on Wyatt's door.

He answered after a few moments, still in the same

fetching costume. This time he stood there, a bottle of orange juice in his hand, a section of paper folded under his arm.

He stared at her, perplexed. And maybe a little ir-ritated. "Yes?"

"Where is she?"

Now he just looked confused. "Who?"

"You know who. Daisy."

"Daisy," he repeated.

"The redhead? Green dress?" Phoebe figured maybe he'd forgotten to ask Daisy's name.

"I don't know where she is," he finally said. "Have you tried her apartment?" He opened the door wider, indicating Phoebe should come all the way in.

She did, intending to conduct a thorough search. Daisy would probably be really mad at her for being so nosy, but someone had to watch out for the woman.

"She's not home," Phoebe said, looking all around. No sign of an overnight guest. No discarded clothing lying around on the living room floor. No breakfast place setting for two at the dining room table.

She turned to face Wyatt. "You were hitting on her at the party last night. You didn't even pay your respects to the hostess, which you should have after you told me you weren't coming. But you didn't waste any time cornering poor Daisy and whisking her off someplace."

"Poor Daisy?" he repeated incredulously.

"She's very vulnerable right now," Phoebe per-sisted. "She doesn't need some wolf twice her age overwhelming her with promises he has no intention of keeping.''

Wyatt narrowed his eyes. "Twice her age? Not unless she's nineteen. Exactly how old do you think I am?''

Phoebe took a deep breath. "All right, the age reference was out of line. I didn't hear you denying you're a wolf, though.''

"Phoebe, look at me. Look me in the eye, because I want to be sure you're listening.''

She didn't want to. Those velvety gray eyes of his saw too much. But she did. Bless it, he was too darn good-looking for anyone's peace of mind, least of all hers.

He took a step closer, until she could feel his body heat. "I did not hit on your friend Daisy. I did not whisk her off anyplace. And though I don't like to gossip, I will tell you that I *did* see her leave the party—with some guy.''

"Who?" The single word dripped with suspicion.

"I have no idea. I don't know anyone here.''

"What did he look like?''

Wyatt shrugged, stepping back and giving them both some much-needed breathing room.

"How should I know? I don't pay that much attention to how guys look.''

"Just women," Phoebe couldn't resist adding.

"Why would you think that?" Wyatt said, sounding genuinely perplexed. He flopped down onto the sofa and started straightening the newspaper that was strewn about. "Did my grandparents tell you I was some sort of lecher?''

"No, no, they've never had anything but nice things to say about you."

"Then what? I've never done anything since I moved here except keep to myself!"

"Well, you work in television," Phoebe said, knowing she sounded lame.

"And that makes me out to nail every female I meet?"

"I'm just going by my personal experience."

Wyatt didn't seem to know what to make of that. He didn't look at her, just kept stacking sections of newspaper together neatly.

"Okay," Phoebe finally said, "maybe I jumped to conclusions a little."

"A little?" He pushed the newspapers aside and leaned back, stretching his arms above his head. "I can assure you, the last thing on my mind right now is adding notches to my bedpost. I have a new job, the kind of opportunity that comes along once in a lifetime, and I have maybe a few weeks at most to prove myself. If the show succeeds, the world is my oyster. If it tanks, I'm back to producing local cooking shows and public service announcements. I spend every waking moment worrying about that damn show."

Phoebe studied Wyatt, really studied him. Suddenly he didn't seem like every other schmoozy show-business guy she'd known. He cared about his work. In fact, it appeared he actually *worked,* rather than taking long expense-account lunches and talking on his cell phone.

"I'm sorry," she said. "I don't know what I was

thinking, or why I said those things." Temporary insanity, maybe.

He smiled at her, though she couldn't imagine why. He should have just thrown her out into the hall on her ear.

"The truth is, Phoebe, I have no use for women right now. But if I did...if I were going to hit on anybody living at Mesa Blue, it would be you. Daisy is pretty, but leggy blondes are more to my taste."

Phoebe's heart slammed into her chest. Had she actually been thinking charitable thoughts about him only moments ago? Had she actually apologized for thinking he was a wolf? He was grinning at her, a grin that would put any wolf at the zoo to shame.

"Thanks just the same," Phoebe said coolly. "As it turns out, I have no use for men at this point in my life. So that works out well, doesn't it?"

Wyatt nodded. "Very convenient."

Something else was going on here, Phoebe thought. He was watching her, as if he expected her to pull a rabbit out of her ear or something.

"So I should just go, I guess."

"Seems we've said all there is to say."

"Well, goodbye, then."

"Goodbye." He picked up a section of newspaper and started reading.

The nerve!

Phoebe finally managed to drag herself out the front door, marveling at her reluctance. She tried to convince herself she'd merely wanted to come up with a zinger of an exit line. But by the time she made it back to her apartment, she had to admit something awful: she'd been tempted by Wyatt's come-on.

She'd been a heartbeat away from meeting his flirtation with one of her own.

She paused a moment, standing just inside the front door, to picture it. "Oh, Wyatt, I'm flattered, but... actually, I find you quite attractive, too," she would say. "But, of course, if you don't have time for women, I understand..." And while she talked, she would slowly unfasten her overalls, first one shoulder, then the other....

Back in the present, she could only gasp at the outrageous turn her little fantasy had taken. "Adelaide Phelps," she said aloud, using the name she'd grown up with, the name no one but her mother even knew about. "That wasn't a flirtation, that was a seduction, and if that's what's on your mind, you better just stay away from Wyatt Madison!"

WYATT TOSSED the newspaper aside, his entire body thrumming with anticipation for something that would never happen.

He ought to be consumed with relief that Phoebe hadn't taken his bait. He'd been testing her with that come-on line. If she'd had any intention of using his show-business connections to revive her career, he'd just given her the perfect opportunity.

But she hadn't responded as predicted. In fact, she'd all but crossed herself and hung garlic around her neck to keep him away. Wait a minute, was garlic for werewolves or vampires?

Well, no matter. She'd made it clear she wanted nothing to do with him. She thought he was *old,* damn it. He was thirty-nine, in the prime of his life. He wasn't old; it was just that Phoebe was young. When he'd been in college, she'd been jumping rope on the playground.

He had to keep reminding himself of things like that. Because he hadn't felt at all relieved when Phoebe had turned her nose up at his flirting. He'd felt keen disappointment. And just what would he have done if she'd responded? He'd like to think he would have politely but firmly sent her home with a pat on the head. Unfortunately, he knew damn well he'd have peeled those overalls right off her, given even half a chance.

"WELL, IF IT ISN'T my three best customers," said George, Phoebe's favorite waiter at The Prickly Pear. The upscale bar and grill was only a few blocks from Mesa Blue, and the three friends ended up here for dinner at least once a week, as did several of their neighbors.

George automatically set drinks in front of Elise, Daisy and Phoebe, already familiar with their habitual choices. The three friends always chose the same table, when it was unoccupied, so George could wait on them.

"Evening, George," Phoebe said with a smile, letting him kiss her on the cheek. Like Jeff, his flirtations were harmless. He had a wife he adored.

"You lovelies want the usual?" George asked.

They all nodded. Chicken Caesar salads all the way around. Their order never varied.

It was two days after Phoebe's last encounter with Wyatt. She'd tried to forget about it, push it out of her mind, but she found herself annoyingly preoccupied with thoughts of what might have happened if she'd reacted differently to his come-on.

Elise made an exaggerated throat-clearing sound. "Will you join us, Phoebe?"

"Huh?"

"You're off in never-never land again," Daisy said.

Elise nudged her. "This is an important occasion, and I want you paying attention."

"Sorry." She focused on Elise. Important? Had she forgotten someone's birthday? "What's going on?"

"Momentous, in fact," Elise said. "You were both very supportive during James's and my…courtship."

"Courtship?" Daisy said dryly. "More like a roller coaster."

"So tonight," Elise continued, ignoring her, "I am officially asking both of you to be bridesmaids."

Phoebe was unexpectedly touched, as Daisy appeared to be. They both jumped out of their chairs to hug their friend.

"I figured with all those sisters, you wouldn't need any more bridesmaids," Phoebe said.

"This is my one and only wedding, and I plan to have as many bridesmaids as I want. Six, so far, and it's not eight only because one of my sisters will be out of the country and another will be eight months' pregnant by September and she refuses to waddle down the aisle."

"I love weddings," Daisy said on a sigh. "I'm really happy for you, Elise, but I wish it were mine."

"We'll have you married off in no time," Elise said. "In fact, there's a new teaching assistant in the Languages Department. Spanish. He's gorgeous, kind of like Antonio Banderas, and he's single.'' Elise pulled a card out of her purse and handed it to Daisy. ''He said for you to call him.''

Daisy took the card without much enthusiasm. ''How old is he?'' she asked suspiciously.

''Oh, I don't know.''

''He's younger than me, I bet,'' Daisy said.

''Maybe a little, but that shouldn't matter. He's very nice, very much a gentleman.''

Daisy sighed. ''I'm reduced to begging for dates with destitute grad students.''

''He's not destitute,'' Elise argued. ''Anyway, the last rich guy you went out with drove you crazy with all his *things*.''

Daisy groaned. ''The dentist. Why do I let you guys keep fixing me up?''

''Because it's a numbers game,'' Elise said. ''You have to kiss a lot of toads before you find the prince. And, anyway, the rejects have single friends.''

''Maybe…'' Phoebe ventured, ''maybe Daisy doesn't want us to fix her up anymore because she found someone on her own.''

''What?'' Daisy said sharply. ''Phoebe, I told you, Wyatt and I are just friends. We talked for about ten minutes, and that was it.''

''Not Wyatt,'' Phoebe said. ''The other guy. The one you left the party with.''

''Oh, do tell,'' Elise said.

Daisy took a long sip of her iced tea. ''So, Elise, have you chosen your colors yet?''

Well, that didn't go over well, Phoebe thought. She'd been hoping to tease Daisy into revealing the identity of the mystery man Wyatt had mentioned.

She figured there would be a simple explanation. But clearly Daisy didn't want to talk about it.

"I'm not sure about colors yet," Elise said, "but I was thinking maybe a pale yellow for the bridesmaid dresses."

"Only if you want me to look like a corpse," Phoebe said flippantly, then wished she'd thought before she'd spoken. Elise should be allowed to pick any color she wanted. It didn't matter that yellow washed out Phoebe's skin and made her hair look like straw.

"I forgot—you do look dreadful in yellow. No offense."

"None taken. Don't worry about that, though. Pick whatever color you like best."

"No, no, I don't want any *Night of the Living Dead* bridesmaids. Maybe pink—"

"Pink? On a redhead?" Daisy said. "Clash city."

"You're right," Elise said. "Well, I'll think some more."

"Let's get back to Wyatt," Daisy said. "What are you going to do about him, Phoebe?"

"Me?" Phoebe hoped her friends couldn't see the sweat popping out on her forehead. "Why would I do anything with him?"

"Because the man is clearly besotted with you," Daisy said. "At the party he was staring at you like a cat eyeing the last sardine."

Chapter Four

Wyatt was having a Tuesday that put all other bad Tuesdays to shame. He was beginning to wonder if he would ever get used to temperamental guests on the show, especially now that he was dealing with so many of them. "Heads Up" wasn't just an ordinary talk show. It dealt with trends—anything cutting edge, from the newest hot movie star to the latest in gene therapy. His hosts—a young, romantically involved couple—were hip and charismatic, and they were adept at getting past both glib sound bites and technobabble. Despite the show's wide-ranging subjects—going against the television industry's niche marketing philosophy—it was drawing a good-size audience from a wide demographic.

But some days, like today, Wyatt had his doubts about whether the show would go on at all. The featured guests, a 16-year-old star of a hot new nighttime soap, gave new meaning to the word *ego*. The show's hosts were engaged in a romantic quarrel, something Wyatt had known would happen eventually, given their volatile personalities.

And now his makeup artist was threatening to quit.

"If that oversexed little snip grabs my breast one more time," Carmen complained, "I'm going to give him a black eye!"

"Carmen, you can't assault our guests, no matter how bad their behavior."

"You wouldn't say that if he groped you!"

"I'll have a talk with him."

"No. I want you to get Jean to do his makeup." Jean was the stylist who did Kelly and Kurt, his hosts.

"Jean has already left for the day," Wyatt pointed out.

"Someone else, then!"

"We all have other jobs to do." Some of which weren't getting done. Tension on the set had a tendency to slow things down.

"Wyatt!" screamed Kelly Cupps, the female half of his hosting team. Wyatt glanced in the direction of the half-hysterical summons. She stood on the set in a robe, hair in curlers, feet bare. "There's no bottled water in my dressing room!"

Wyatt put a hand to Carmen's shoulder. "Carmen, please, I just need you to—"

She jumped away from him. "You men are all the same, always touching, touching, touching. Well, I'm through! I quit!" And she did.

Wyatt stared after her, incredulous.

"Wyatt, what about my water!" Kelly screamed.

Damn it, he was the producer, not an errand boy. He grabbed one of the grips. "Do me a big favor and get the Aqua Queen some bottled water?"

"That violates union rules, man. Sorry."

Wyatt got the water himself, out of his own stash

in his office. Then he called around and tried to find another makeup artist. But his contacts in Phoenix were limited. He simply hadn't lived here long enough. Jean didn't answer when he paged her. He put out calls to a couple of others he found in his director's Rolodex, but by sixty minutes to airtime he still didn't have anyone to do his guests' makeup.

He was about to borrow Kelly's suitcase of cosmetics and do the job himself, when he remembered someone else he knew who did makeovers. What was the name of that spa where she worked? Sunshine…no, Sunrise.

On impulse, he dialed Information.

PHOEBE CAREFULLY REMOVED electric rollers from the fragile, auburn-tinted hair of one of her clients, Mrs. Cooper.

"I just don't know, honey," the sixty-something woman said, frowning into the mirror. "I'm not sure this color is me. I used to be a redhead, you know."

Phoebe knew. Mrs. Cooper had informed her of that fact several times a day last week while Phoebe tried every hair color on the shelf to please her.

"Why don't you try living with it for a few days?" Phoebe suggested. "It looks good with your coloring."

"I'll decide what looks good, missy," Mrs. Cooper said curtly. "I'm the one paying a thousand dollars a day."

Phoebe stifled a groan. Not all the rich ladies she worked with had this kind of attitude. In fact, most of them were very nice, and sometimes quite gracious when Phoebe worked her magic on them. She firmly believed that every woman, no matter how seemingly plain, had beautiful qualities that could be accentuated with the right hairstyle or makeup choices. Some of her clients were downright astounded when she brought their inner beauty to the surface.

Then there were the Mrs. Coopers of the world, who would never be beautiful because they never smiled. They treated Phoebe like a servant with no feelings.

Phoebe's intercom buzzed, dispelling her dismal thoughts. *"Phone for you"* came the voice of Pam, Sunrise's receptionist.

"I don't take calls during appointments," Phoebe gently reminded Pam. She also firmly believed all her clients—even Mrs. Cooper—deserved a hundred percent of her attention.

"I know, and I'm sorry," Pam said, sounding anxious. "But he said it's an emergency."

Phoebe's heart skipped a beat. All she could think about was her mother, her only living relative. Olga Phelps was healthy as a horse, as far as Phoebe knew. Had something happened to her? Phoebe apologized to the tightly frowning Mrs. Cooper and picked up the phone.

"Phoebe Lane."

"Phoebe, thank God. It's Wyatt Madison."

Now her heart went into overdrive. Why would he be calling her? "It's not—I mean, your grandparents are okay, aren't they?" she asked.

"Yes, yes, they're fine. I'm calling because... How would you like to make a fast three hundred bucks?"

"What?"

"Whoa, let me rephrase that. I need a makeup artist. Mine just walked out, and my show goes on the air in forty-five minutes. You're my last resort."

Phoebe's first instinct was to say no. She'd left the entertainment industry three years ago without a backward glance, and she had no intention of making a comeback. But the real reason she wanted to say no was that she didn't need any more excuses to hang out with Wyatt. The man drove her crazy. Knowing he lived and slept just two doors down from her was bad enough, even if she didn't see him very often. But now that she knew he thought of her as a "leggy blonde," things were ten times worse.

"I'll make it four hundred," he said, when her extended silence became uncomfortable.

"To do what, exactly?" She couldn't believe she was even considering his offer.

"Make up our guests. We have two. Shouldn't take longer than thirty minutes. Kelly and Kurt already have their makeup on," he added.

She supposed she should know who Kelly and Kurt were, but she seldom watched TV. No time.

"Five hundred," Wyatt said, sounding desperate. "Final offer."

"I'll do it on one condition," she finally agreed, unable to say no to him. Shoot, five hundred bucks for less than an hour's work wasn't something she could afford to walk away from. Her financial needs were modest, given that she owned both her car and her condo outright. But the spa didn't pay her that much, and school was expensive.

"Name it," Wyatt said.

"I want your promise there'll be no more 'leggy blonde' comments. I promised myself when I left L.A. that I would never again—"

"Oh, hell, I didn't mean that. Sorry if it upset you or anything. I was testing you."

Well, that was a new twist, Phoebe thought. She'd heard all kinds of excuses when a man tried to save face, but none had ever claimed to be testing her.

"When Daisy told me you were an actress," he explained, "I thought for sure you'd try to use me to somehow revive your career."

"What on earth would make you think—"

"Past experience. The same thing that makes you think I'm out to jump women."

Point taken, she thought with a small pang of guilt.

"You're safe with me, I promise," he added.

Phoebe was annoyed by the sense of disappointment she felt. Did he find her totally unappealing?

"Will you do it?" he asked again.

"Did I pass your test?"

He chuckled. "With flying colors. Been a long time since anyone so thoroughly bruised my ego."

"Then I'll come to the station immediately."

She actually heard his sigh of relief before they hung up. If she'd thought for a moment he was anything but sincere in his plight, she'd never have agreed to help. Helen and Rolland Madison would be really hurt if she turned her back on their precious grandson when he was in a jam.

"Mrs. Cooper, I'm—" She stopped. Mrs. Cooper was gone. Phoebe had been so wrapped up in her conversation with Wyatt, she hadn't even noticed her neglected client getting up and leaving. Phoebe was about to go in search of the woman to apologize, when the door to her treatment room flew open without a knock. Her boss, Madelaine Fitzhugh, burst in looking as if she wanted to chew on something firm— like Phoebe's butt.

"What did you do to Mrs. Cooper?" Madelaine demanded, her arms crossed beneath her improbably large breasts.

"Aside from dying her hair for the fifth time?"

"Don't be snippy with me, Phoebe."

Phoebe hated being spoken to like a sixth grader caught smoking in the bathroom, but she did her best to screen the irritation out of her voice. "I took a phone call. Three minutes, max."

"She said you were gushing with your boyfriend."

Phoebe almost laughed. What on earth had given Mrs. Cooper that idea? "No. It was a friend, and I've got to help him with an emergency." She peeled off her smock.

"You're leaving?"

"I don't have another client until four o'clock," Phoebe assured her boss. And she was paid by the client, not the hour.

"But I might need you. Flora Cummings wants a manicure at one."

"Madelaine, you know I can't work from eleven to three."

"Except in special circumstances. This is special."

"I need twenty-four hours' warning. That's our deal." Anyway, Phoebe had her organic chemistry test at two. No way was she giving any manicures this afternoon. She gathered up her makeup and arranged it in a big silver case.

Madelaine narrowed her eyes. "Who are you working for? You did sign a non-compete agreement."

"It's not a spa. It's for a TV show."

Madelaine tried to look nonchalant, but Phoebe could tell she was angry. She stepped toward the lighted wall mirror, picked up one of Phoebe's brushes and fussed with her bangs.

"Well, between this TV gig and your other mysterious comings and goings, sounds like you don't really need the Sunrise Spa. So don't bother coming back."

Phoebe was incredulous. "Oh, Madelaine, don't go all melodramatic on me." But she was talking to thin air. Before she had even finished voicing her objection, Madelaine had gone.

"Great," Phoebe grumbled, hoisting her case and her purse and heading for the nearest exit. Something else to feel irritated with Wyatt for. He'd gotten her fired. Indirectly, of course, but still...

She stopped that line of thinking. She'd gotten herself fired. She'd long ago shed the victim mentality learned from her mother. She was responsible for taking Wyatt's call, for ignoring Mrs. Cooper and for being "snippy." She could always go back to work for Weldon's Department Store, passing out perfume samples until she found something better—though the pay was dreadful. But maybe she could at least negotiate regular hours. Being at Madelaine's beck and call had wreaked havoc on her studying.

All that rationalization didn't stop her from feeling annoyed.

IT WAS FIFTEEN MINUTES to airtime when Phoebe finally walked through the studio door. Wyatt had alerted security of her imminent arrival and instructed them to give her a visitor's badge and escort her posthaste to the set. The moment he saw her, he felt a tremendous rush of relief coupled with a bothersome surge of lust. But what healthy male wouldn't lust after her? he reasoned. Dressed in a snug knit top and even snugger black pants, walking with that graceful, loose-limbed gait of hers, she was an erotic dream waiting to happen.

She looked around, finally catching his gaze and waving an acknowledgment. She started toward him, and he met her halfway. *About damn time,* he wanted to say. But he knew that was his own anxiety talking. She'd no doubt gotten here as quickly as she could, and since she was his last hope of preventing this show from self-destructing, he sure as hell couldn't afford to tick her off.

"I'm sorry it took me so long," she said breathlessly. "Traffic was terrible."

"That's okay." He took her heavy case, grabbed her elbow and steered her toward a hallway that started at the back of the studio and extended past dressing rooms and offices. He tried not to think about the fact that even Phoebe's elbow was sexy.

When they reached one of the dressing rooms, he tapped, and a female voice told them to come in.

Wyatt opened the door and led Phoebe inside. "Phoebe, this is Muriel Topper. She wrote—"

"That diet book!" Phoebe said, sounding surprised and pleased. "We sell it at the spa where I work, and we can't keep enough copies in stock. I'm Phoebe Lane."

Muriel, gracefully thin and quite beautiful for a seventy-year-old, smiled and extended a hand. "Nice to meet you. Hope you've got something in that case of yours for these bags under my eyes."

"In fact, I do. But I don't notice any bags," she quickly added.

"You only have about fifteen minutes to get Muriel ready," Wyatt cautioned. "Then I need you to step next door and start on our other guest. He won't be on 'til nine-thirty."

"No problem," Phoebe said breezily, already opening her case and selecting sponges, brushes and various colors of foundation and eye pencil. "Who's the other guest?"

"An actor," Wyatt answered.

Phoebe frowned. "That narrows it down."

"Taylor Shad."

She froze. "You're joking. This is a joke, right?"

"'Fraid not. You know him?"

"Well, yeah. He played my little brother on 'Skin Deep.'"

"Then you all should have a lot to catch up on. Yell if you need anything."

Wyatt got out of there. The expression on Phoebe's face was trouble. He could tell she didn't like Shad—who did?—and he was half afraid she might refuse to do the kid's makeup. Better to not even give her the chance to slither out of her commitment.

"THAT SHAD KID is a real piece of work, isn't he?" Muriel commented, as Phoebe touched up her hair.

Phoebe had immediately liked Muriel. She'd written an easy-to-understand nutrition book for senior women, and it was selling like snow cones on a hot Phoenix street corner.

"You've met him?" Phoebe asked.

"When I first got here. He said, 'Hey, mama, you don't look bad for an old broad.'"

Phoebe gasped. "Sounds like he's even worse than when I knew him three years ago. Back then he used to pinch bottoms, snap bra straps and tell dirty jokes."

"Well, I don't want to alarm you," Muriel said, "but I think Taylor Shad is the reason the makeup artist quit in a huff."

"Oh, really?" And Wyatt hadn't even warned her about him. Well, the little snot sure wouldn't bully *her* into quitting, she thought. She'd been harassed by worse than him.

An intern came to get Muriel. Phoebe, pleased with how the older woman's makeup and hair had turned out, wished her good luck, then packed up her supplies to move to Taylor's dressing room. How old would he be now? About sixteen, Phoebe calculated. She hadn't kept up with his career, or anyone else's for that matter. She hardly ever watched TV or went to the movies.

She knocked on Taylor's door.

"Enter" came the imperious response.

She cautiously opened the door. Taylor Shad looked more man than boy, now.

His eyes lit up with surprise. "Well, I'll be damned, if it isn't Vanessa Vance."

"Phoebe Lane," she corrected him, irritated he didn't remember her real name. As she stepped into the room, she purposely left the door open.

"I didn't know you were gonna be on 'Heads Up,' too." Then he spied her makeup case. "Oh, don't tell me. You do makeup now?"

"Yup." She set her case on the vanity and mechanically went through the motions of selecting colors and applicators.

He hooted with laughter. "Kind of a comedown, huh, sister dearest?"

She didn't respond.

"Man, oh, man. I knew nobody picked you up after Vanessa got killed off, but I can't believe you sank *this* low. Tell me it's a joke."

Phoebe gritted her teeth. "I got out of acting because I didn't like it. I enjoy doing makeup."

"Yeah, right," Taylor said. "How much do you get paid for this grunt work?"

"Today, five hundred dollars an hour," Phoebe said, just to shut him up.

It didn't work. "On my new show, I get fifty thousand dollars an episode."

"How nice for you." Even if he was telling the truth, which she doubted, she was unimpressed. "Close your eyes, please." She turned toward him with a sponge full of foundation makeup.

Taylor complied, and for a few moments Phoebe

thought he might be quiet and cooperate. No such luck.

"You smell great," he said.

"Thanks," she replied, no emotion in her voice.

"I bet you taste good, too."

"You'll never know, will you?"

"All the guys on 'Skin Deep' had a running bet about you, you know."

"No, I didn't know," Phoebe said, bored. "Lift your chin." She gingerly applied makeup to his neck.

"We were betting whether your breasts were real or not."

Phoebe didn't reply. Let him wonder all he wanted.

"Mark said they were, but Vinnie said they weren't."

"As if either of them would know." She tried not to let it get to her that a couple of low-life technicians on the "Skin Deep" set claimed they had intimate knowledge of her body. "Turn to the right."

By the time she finished his foundation, she thought the discussion was over. But he wouldn't drop it.

"You look like you've gained weight."

"I've been working out."

"You must have pretty good muscle tone." He grabbed her butt. "Yeah, you do."

She gently but firmly grasped his hand and removed it from her person. "Don't touch me again, or I'll make you look like a female impersonator." This was dreadful. She wouldn't feel a bit guilty about taking five hundred dollars from Wyatt. At least at Sunrise her clients didn't grope her.

"Oh, now, Vanessa—"

"Phoebe. Ms. Lane, to you."

"You're obviously much too tense. What you need is a good massage." As if he had a perfect right to, he placed his hands on her breasts and started squeezing.

Phoebe reacted with pure instinct. She slapped him.

He let go, but immediately came out of his chair, pure rage in his eyes. He pushed her up against the wall of his dressing room and pinned her there. "You audacious, two-bit, has-been actress," he hissed in her face. "You are gonna be real sorry you did that."

Phoebe was only a little scared. She'd been through similar scenarios before. The door to the dressing room was open, and if she screamed really loud someone would come running. But she preferred to deal with this her own way rather than causing trouble on the set of Wyatt's show. She could knee Taylor in the groin or—

All at once he let her go. Phoebe breathed a sigh of relief—until she realized Wyatt had Taylor by the scruff of the neck and was shaking him the way a terrier would a rat.

"What the hell do you think you're doing!" Wyatt bellowed. Taylor swung his arms ineffectually and squealed for Wyatt to let him go. Wyatt wound up like he was going to punch Taylor in the face, but Phoebe grabbed his arm to prevent it.

"No, Wyatt! You'll get sued!"

"Damn right he will!" Taylor agreed, no doubt sensing Phoebe wouldn't allow any further violence.

"For defending my employee against sexual assault?'' Wyatt said, gradually loosening his hold on Taylor. "I don't think so. That's not the kind of publicity you want.''

Taylor straightened his clothes, never taking his eyes off Wyatt. After backing a safe distance away, he looked back at Phoebe. "Let's just finish the makeup. I'm on in fifteen minutes.''

"No, you're not,'' Wyatt said, picking up the phone. He pushed a button and spoke into the receiver. "I need Security in the dressing room area.''

"I'm not going on?'' Taylor asked.

"No. I don't give free publicity to sexual predators.''

"Give me a break, man. I wasn't doing anything she didn't invite me to do.''

The excuse sickened Phoebe. How many times had she heard some guy swear she was "coming on to'' him? Still, she didn't want Wyatt to get sued over this.

"It's okay, Wyatt,'' she said quietly. "I appreciate your concern, but it's not that big a deal. Taylor just got a little carried away.''

Wyatt flashed her a look that was part anger, part sympathy. "I saw what was happening,'' he said, just as quietly.

Two security guards appeared at the door. Wyatt motioned them inside. "Escort Mr. Shad and his entourage to their limousine.''

"I'll sue you, man!'' Taylor said. "We have a contract.''

Wyatt just nodded to the guards. In moments each

had one of Taylor's arms and they were dragging him out the dressing room door.

"You didn't have to do that," Phoebe said, when she and Wyatt were alone. "I had it under control."

"That's not what it looked like to me."

"I was just trying to decide whether to scream or knee him in the groin." But her trembling gave her away. Taylor Shad had scared her worse than she'd realized.

"Phoebe."

Her name on his lips sounded like a caress. He gently took her arm and led her and her shaky knees to the chair Taylor had just vacated. Without another word, he handed her a tissue. That was when she realized she was crying.

"Do you want to press charges against him?" Wyatt asked. "Just say the word, and I'll call the cops."

"Heavens, no." Phoebe blotted carefully at her tears, trying not to smear her own makeup. "But if he sues you, I'll testify."

"He won't sue me. The contract never guaranteed he'd actually get on the air."

"And how are you going to fill up the other half of the show?" She turned toward the TV mounted in a corner of the room, where even now one of the hosts was promising an appearance by a hot young star.

"Contingency plan. But I'd better go put it in motion. You sure you're okay?"

Phoebe smiled and nodded, feeling a surge of gratitude toward Wyatt. He hadn't once insinuated she was to blame for the incident. A lot of people assumed that blond hair and a *C* cup were an automatic invitation.

After he'd gone, she drank some water and repaired her makeup. Feeling more herself, she wandered out to the set to watch, finding a stool well out of the way to perch on.

During the commercial break Wyatt was all over the studio, briefing his hosts on the change of plans, ordering someone to move a light, explaining to the audience that they wouldn't be seeing Taylor Shad, after all. With calm efficiency he took what could have been a monumental disaster and turned it into a minor annoyance. Phoebe caught herself thinking that if Wyatt had been producing "Skin Deep," the show might have fared much better.

The second half of the show went on as if they'd planned it that way all along. The hosts brought out a board game that was sweeping college campuses, inviting a couple of preselected audience members to participate. The results were hilarious.

Wyatt came and stood next to her. "You okay?" he asked, his voice full of concern.

"I'm fine."

"I'm really sorry it happened."

"It's not your fault. How could you have known Taylor would assault me?"

"What do you think happened to my regular makeup artist?"

"Oh."

"I should have sent someone in there with you. Or, at least, warned you."

"You had a few other things on your mind."

"No, that's not it. I didn't tell you because I was afraid you'd quit, too."

Phoebe had to admit one thing: Wyatt was refreshingly honest.

"Forget about it, okay? It's not the first time someone made an unwanted pass at me, and it probably won't be the last."

But she knew the pass wouldn't come from Wyatt. Ever since he'd rescued her from Taylor, he'd taken great pains to behave with exaggerated professionalism. In fact, he acted as if he thought she might shatter.

Too bad, she caught herself thinking. If Wyatt ever tried to kiss her, it wouldn't once occur to her to knee him in the groin.

Chapter Five

The commercial break ended, and as the last segment of the show aired, Wyatt unobtrusively studied Phoebe, wondering what all she'd been through. By her own admission, this wasn't the first time someone had tried to force her into something. She tried to pretend it was no big deal, but he'd seen the raw fear in her eyes when Taylor had had her pinned against the wall. He'd seen the relief when he'd pulled Taylor off her. And he'd seen the sadness just now.

She'd been through hell.

Now all Wyatt could think about was making sure nothing bad ever touched her again. He felt responsible for this morning's disaster. He owed her.

The show ended, and everyone agreed they'd pulled it off. His hosts had come up with a plausible excuse for Taylor Shad's absence, and the game had worked out better than expected. But instead of taking care of the million details in preparation for tomorrow's show, Wyatt followed Phoebe into the dressing room where she'd gone to gather up her things.

"So, what did you think?" he asked.

"I think you're doing a great job."

Her praise pleased him all out of proportion. "Would you like to come back?"

Her hands stilled. "You mean, to do makeup?"

"My regular person quit. I need to hire someone, and you obviously know your stuff." He could get used to being around her, he decided. "I wouldn't blame you if you weren't interested, after what happened—"

"Would you please forget about that? I don't want you thinking of me as some kind of victim, or a fragile little thing that needs protecting."

Hell, that's exactly how he was thinking of her. "I won't mention it again." But he wouldn't forget it.

"Good." She smiled. "I'm a lot tougher than I look. Don't forget, I swam with the Hollywood sharks. Taylor Shad was just a minnow."

"What about the job?"

She hesitated. "What are the hours, and what does it pay?"

He told her. She dropped a makeup brush. "No kidding?"

He suspected it was more than she made at the spa.

"What about weekends?" she asked.

"No weekends."

"That'd be perfect," she murmured. Then, louder, she said, "No, I really don't think—" She stopped. "What am I saying? Of course, I'll take it."

Wyatt's relief was palpable. "I assume you'll need to give notice at the spa. I'm sure I can find a substitute—"

"I can start tomorrow. My boss at Sunrise fired me this morning."

"Why?" he asked.

"Because I was coming here. Because I refused to let her push me around."

"I got you fired?" It just got worse and worse. His debt to her kept growing.

"No, you gave me a great new job. Where do I sign up?"

Wyatt took her to Personnel, where she got some forms to fill out. He also got a five-hundred dollar check cut for that morning's work. Then suddenly, at eleven-fifteen, she looked at her watch and got a panicky expression in her eyes.

"Oh, my gosh, I have to go," she said breathlessly. She grabbed her case and her purse, then pulled the visitor badge off her collar and handed it to him.

"You have another job or something?" he asked, keeping pace with her, as she headed for the station's front doors.

"Or something. What time tomorrow?"

"We'll talk about it later."

Then she peeled out of the studio as if her pants were on fire. Wyatt sat down in the nearest chair, feeling like he'd been run over by a bulldozer. Had he just hired Phoebe Lane to be on the staff of his show? His grandparents would be pleased. But he would see her every day. Which meant that every day he would have to resist his attraction to her. He knew better than to have a relationship with someone on his staff.

Just as well, he tried to tell himself. He didn't need a woman in his life right now. Anyway, Phoebe had made it abundantly clear she wasn't interested in him, either. As pretty as she was, she was probably used to setting boundaries in clear terms, up front. If she didn't, she'd be hit from all sides.

WHEN PHOEBE got home from her classes that night, she noticed Wyatt's car in his carport. That in itself was unusual—he was almost never home. Even more unusual was the note on her door from him. "Call me when you get in—we need to discuss tomorrow's show. Wyatt."

"And what's wrong with leaving a message on my answering machine?" she murmured as she let herself into her apartment. But she was coming to realize Wyatt never did anything the ordinary way. He was altogether unpredictable.

She was tired and achey and out of sorts. Her organic chemistry test hadn't gone well, and she had another test tomorrow—calculus—that she had to study for tonight. Having to squeeze in a meeting with her new boss should be making her feel even crankier.

But she looked forward to seeing Wyatt. Normally she didn't like it when an employer infringed on her personal time. But for some reason, she didn't begrudge Wyatt his request. She went straight to the phone and called him.

"Phoebe."

He sounded pleased to hear from her.

"You rushed away so quickly today I didn't have a chance to brief you about tomorrow's guests. You want to go out for coffee, and I can give you the rundown?"

Phoebe didn't want to be difficult, but going out didn't sound like much fun. She'd been gone all day, and more than anything she wanted to put on her fluffy robe and slippers, and curl into her beanbag chair with her books. "Why don't you come over here?" she said brightly. "I'll put a pot of coffee on." She would need it for the late night of studying she had planned.

"If you'd rather. See you in a few."

Phoebe put on the coffee, then quickly picked up her apartment, careful to stow her schoolbooks in the bedroom. She'd told almost no one about trying to get a college degree. Daisy and Elise knew, and Wyatt's grandparents, but they'd all been sworn to secrecy.

After moving to Phoenix, she'd gone to a career counselor and taken some tests to find out what, aside from acting and makeup, she might be good at. She'd been floored when she got her test results back. She'd made almost a perfect score on the SAT, and the IQ test had placed her at near-genius level.

"My mother would faint" was the first thing Phoebe told the counselor. Olga, who had immigrated to America from Denmark when she was a child, had never pressured Phoebe to make good grades. "God did not give you that gorgeous face and body so you could become a nuclear physicist," Olga had said more than once. "You've got everything you need to become a movie star or land a rich husband, or both."

Olga, despite looking very much like her daughter, had done neither. Phoebe's factory-worker father had disappeared when she was three, and Olga had never remarried, though she'd tried awfully hard and was still trying. As for show business, the pinnacle of Olga's career had been when she played a Swedish maid for two weekends at a dinner theater.

That didn't stop her from having sky-high hopes for her daughter—acting classes, dance classes, speech classes to get rid of that New Jersey accent, and beauty school, just in case.

For a while, Phoebe had bought into Olga's fantasy. She'd skated through high school with straight *C*s because she figured she wouldn't need an education. Later, after Phoebe moved to L.A. and changed her name, all of Olga's dreams for her daughter seemed to be coming true.

But Phoebe's success had been fleeting, a lucky first break that didn't lead to much of anything. Olga had been crushed when Phoebe had announced she was leaving Hollywood and giving up show business. Her worst disappointment was that Phoebe hadn't married some rich movie producer or become Mrs. Brad Pitt.

Phoebe's feet were now more firmly planted than her mother's had ever been. But she still had a hard time believing she was smart. That was why she told very few people of her career aspirations. Because what if the test results were wrong? What if she flunked out? She would feel like a complete fool.

Wyatt was the last person she would tell. It was much easier if he continued to think of her as a blond beautician. Then she wouldn't have to live up to any unrealistic expectations.

When she let Wyatt in a few minutes later, she realized her apartment was clean but that she was a mess. She probably hadn't so much as glanced in a mirror since noon.

"Help yourself to some coffee," she said. "I'm going to change into more comfortable clothes."

Wyatt's soft chuckles followed her down the hallway toward her bedroom. She stepped inside the room, closed the door, then put her face in her hands. Had she actually just told Wyatt Madison she was going to slip into something more comfortable?

WYATT TOOK A FEW SECONDS to fantasize about what outfit Phoebe might change into. A negligee? A net cat suit? Yeah, right. He'd thumbed through one too many Victoria's Secret catalogs. He'd be lucky if she didn't return in a flannel granny gown. He'd learned over the years that was how most women defined *comfortable*.

When he'd visited her apartment before, he'd been too busy fighting back the flood waters to notice much about it. Now he paid attention.

The decor seemed a reflection of Phoebe, he decided. The colors were delicate—peach, yellow, pale aqua—but the white leather sofa was functional and sturdy-looking. Nothing about the apartment screamed professional decorator, yet Phoebe obviously had a feel for comfort and practicality. The oatmeal carpet was thick and soft, but it wouldn't soil easily. She didn't have a lot of cluttery knickknacks that would require dusting.

She did have books, a whole bookshelf full of them. Curious, he walked over to it and perused her titles.

They surprised him a little. He might have expected the romance novels and the few self-help gems. But a biography of Madame Curie, and Stephen Hawking's *A Short History of the Universe* were completely unexpected. He couldn't imagine Phoebe reading physics. Maybe they were just for show. He knew people who bought intelligent-sounding titles and stuck them on their coffee tables just to throw visitors off.

Then a title caught his eye. The book was sitting crossways on top of a row of magazines, so apparently she'd been reading it recently. And the title made his throat close up: *2001 Ways to Wed.*

So, Phoebe was looking for a husband.

He might have guessed. She was that age when women, understandably, started thinking about having babies. He knew now, after reading her employment forms, that she was twenty-eight. But whatever advice she was getting out of that book, she wasn't acting obvious. In fact, he distinctly remembered her saying she didn't have time for a man.

Maybe that was part of the plan.

He couldn't resist flipping through the book. The chapter names were intriguing: "Dating and Mating in the Workplace"; "Don't Forget Your Neighbors"; "What Your Mother Never Told You"; "Bars and Why You Can't Find A Good Man At One"; "Work On Yourself Before You Work on Him."

Phoebe had actually written notes in the margin. She was serious about this, then.

He looked closer at the chapter on neighbors. Was that his name scribbled at the top of one page? He never found out for sure, because he heard her bedroom door open. He quickly closed the book and replaced it on the shelf, then sat down on the sofa and tried to look bored.

The moment Phoebe reentered the living room, Wyatt was forced to abandon any notions he had that

Phoebe was out to snag him as a husband. She'd put on a worn pair of baggy gray sweats and slicked her hair into a no-frills ponytail. She'd also taken off her makeup.

Damn if she still didn't look sexy. She was the only woman he'd ever met who could make such a get-up look enticing. But she didn't seem to be doing it on purpose.

"Coffee?" she asked.

"I don't drink coffee. But please, go ahead." He followed her into the kitchen.

"How about juice?" she asked. "Orange? Cran-apple?"

"Orange would be good."

Wyatt's mind was still on one question that begged to be answered: If Phoebe Lane was looking for a husband, why had she eliminated him from the running? It might be because he'd proved himself a grumpy recluse, but he didn't think that was it. He'd explained to her why he was working so hard, and she'd seemed to understand.

What, then? He was single—never married, in fact—so she wouldn't have to deal with any baggage. He was gainfully employed and financially sound. Of course, she hadn't asked to see last year's tax return, but she would know just from the kind of job he had and the car he drove that he had a bit of disposable income.

He might not be cover-boy material, but he had an okay face, all his teeth and a body that reflected the fact that he worked out.

Did she just not like him? Maybe he was too old for her. She'd made a big deal about his age. But he

knew what was in these how-to-find-a-husband
books. His insatiable curiosity had led him to read
articles in *Cosmopolitan* when no one was looking.
The advice was always the same: Don't rule out any
guy until you get to know him.

Phoebe hardly knew him at all.

His competitive instincts rose to the surface. Did
she have her eye on someone else? Where had she
disappeared to all day today? And, damn it, what was
not to like about him?

The decision was made. He would charm the socks
off Phoebe. Nothing else, just her socks. He didn't
want to marry her, didn't want to lead her on. But he
didn't like being dismissed. He would at least show
her he had worthwhile qualities.

"So, tell me about tomorrow's show," she asked,
as they moved into the small kitchen.

"It's a little more complicated than today's was.
We're doing a fashion segment with clothes made out
of recycled tires—"

"Tires?"

"Yes. We have four models coming in, plus two
additional guests, which means a lot of makeup. I'll
need you at the studio by six."

He expected her to groan, but she just nodded.

"You did warn me there would be some early
mornings required. That's fine. How is the rest of the
week shaping up?"

As they talked about upcoming shows and waited
for the coffee to finish brewing, Wyatt's mind
churned. What would a woman like Phoebe respond
to? Certainly not compliments about her looks. She
probably heard how beautiful she was night and day.

She definitely wouldn't enjoy a physical come-on, not after what had happened to her earlier today. So massages were out.

Power. Would she like that? But somehow he couldn't imagine himself dangling his authority over her, ordering her around. Besides, she might quit.

With a shrug, he decided he would just have to be his usual charming self.

PHOEBE POURED Wyatt a big glass of juice, then herself a cup of coffee. Her kitchen seemed far too small with the two of them standing in it.

He looked great, just fabulous. It seemed every time she saw him he was *more* attractive. She couldn't believe she'd thought he couldn't dress well. Tonight he was wearing a nice pair of jeans and a crisp, blue-striped button-down. Very un-Hollywood, and she loved it. She'd seen enough black turtlenecks in L.A. to last her a lifetime.

She was the one who looked as if she ought to be begging for spare change on the nearest street corner. But she'd dressed like this on purpose, downplaying her physical assets, hoping that by doing so she would guarantee that at least one of them would remain unattracted.

With their beverages of choice, Wyatt and Phoebe returned to the living room. Wyatt sat on the couch. Phoebe put her coffee on the coffee table, grabbed a notebook and pen, and sank into a beanbag chair a safe distance from him.

They spent the next few minutes just talking about the show. Wyatt explained more about his philosophy as producer and his aspirations for the show's future, providing little bits of information about the other staff members. He began to relax, and Phoebe found herself wondering if this was the same remote, austere man who hadn't even bothered to crawl out from under the sink the first time she'd encountered him.

This was the Wyatt his grandparents had told her about—funny, charming, intelligent. He treated her with respect, yet, she knew, he was aware of her as a woman, too. The combination was intoxicating.

Wyatt was the kind of man, she decided, that she'd once aspired to lure into marriage. The kind her mother would love as a son-in-law. In another time and place, she would have flirted with him. She would have used everything in her feminine arsenal to get to him—sexy clothing, perfume, body language.

But that was the old Phoebe, the one who thought her looks were her ticket to whatever she wanted. Things were different now. She had no time for a man in her life. She had career goals that would demand a hundred percent of her concentration.

And Wyatt Madison was her boss.

She'd learned a long time ago that involving herself with a producer was a terrible strategy, a one-way ticket to a bad rep. In Hollywood—and perhaps in Wyatt's circles, too—there was no such thing as innocent flirting.

So Wyatt was off-limits. Absolutely. But resisting him wasn't going to be easy.

As they relaxed into the conversation, they ended up sitting on the floor in front of the coffee table. Wyatt was sketching a picture of the elaborate set he wanted to build for "Heads Up."

"The set we're using now is actually an old relic

from some kids' talk show WBZZ did a few years ago. They weren't willing to put much money into upgrading it. But if the show reaches a certain audience share by the end of April, I get to build a whole new set, whatever I want.''

''I have the greatest idea!'' she said, suddenly inspired.

''Let's hear it.''

''Redecorate your set on a regular basis. Solicit ideas from interior decorators all over the country. Pick a new one, say, once a month. Whatever one you pick redecorates the set—completely at his or her own expense—in exchange for prominent credit and a ten-minute guest shot.''

Wyatt smiled uncertainly. ''We might end up with some pretty weird sets.''

''You give them the basic parameters so that the set is always—''

She gestured excitedly, knocking Wyatt's glass of orange juice squarely into his lap.

For a moment she just stared in horror. How could she have been so clumsy? With all the ballet classes she'd taken, she wasn't normally prone to klutzy moves.

''Uh,'' Wyatt said.

Phoebe hopped into action. ''Don't move. I'll fix it.'' She jumped up and ran to the kitchen, grabbed about twenty paper towels off her roll, and ran back. She knelt down and started daubing at the sodden orange stain on the front of his shirt and jeans. ''I'm so sorry. I don't know how I could have…''

She lost her train of thought when she realized exactly where she was pressing her wad of paper towels.

Wyatt looked at her strangely. Her gaze locked with his, and though she told herself to move away, she couldn't.

"I'm sorry," she said again, only it came out as a hoarse whisper.

"So am I."

She had no conscious memory of who moved next, but they ended up kissing. Maybe he fell back, maybe she pushed him—but she was leaning against his chest, his arms around her, their mouths locked in the most intoxicating kiss Phoebe had ever experienced. He tasted like orange juice, sweet and tart.

She knew it was wrong, knew it was stupid, but she could no more stop than she could shoot out the stars. She kept promising herself just a few more seconds, because it felt so good, but the longer the embrace lasted, the less she wanted to end it.

He pulled the elastic band from her hair, letting the white-gold strands spill over both of them, burying his hands in it.

Gently rolling her onto her back, he slanted his mouth over hers, escalating the kiss. She touched the hard muscles in his back, marveling at how they bunched and relaxed beneath her hands when he shifted positions slightly.

She heard a noise and realized it had come from her, a soft mewling like a kitten, audible evidence of the passion he so effortlessly generated in her.

Abruptly he pulled away.

"Phoebe…" he said on an agonized groan. He lay on his back, breathing rapidly. "Damn it, what the hell just happened?"

Phoebe wished she had an answer. All she knew

was that it was a colossal mistake—one she wanted to repeat, immediately. But glancing over at Wyatt, she saw that there would be no more kissing. Unlike her, he'd come to his senses.

She sat up slowly and pushed her disheveled hair out of her face, feeling dizzy and disoriented. If she didn't put some distance between herself and Wyatt, she might do something that would jeopardize not only her nifty new job, but also her peace of mind.

She grabbed the wad of paper towels and dropped it onto his stomach. "Maybe you'd better clean up your own clothes."

He clutched the paper towels, but otherwise didn't move. He looked completely dazed. Surely one little kiss—okay, one *big* kiss—from her hadn't done that to him?

Before she could lose her determination, she pushed herself onto her feet, fighting light-headedness. Somehow, she had to get their relationship back on a professional footing.

"It's late. I'm going to bed." And just to be sure he didn't misunderstand her, she added, "You can see yourself out."

She marched out of the living room, down the hall and into her bedroom, before she changed her mind and dragged him with her.

Chapter Six

Wyatt lay on Phoebe's living room floor a few more seconds before he was able to summon the strength to sit up. He blotted his clothes, then raised himself onto his knees and daubed at a few drops of orange juice that had hit the carpet. He'd been right: her carpet didn't stain easily.

Moving mechanically, he took his O.J. glass and her cup to the kitchen and rinsed them in the sink. He threw away the paper towels. He switched off her coffeemaker. All the while, he was listening, half hoping he would hear Phoebe's bedroom door open. Praying it wouldn't. Because he wouldn't be strong enough to resist if she changed her mind about continuing what they'd started.

But all was silent.

He turned off her lights and left. It wasn't until he was safely in his apartment that he shook off his numbness and realized fully what had just happened. When he did, he was nearly overwhelmed with self-disgust.

Only this morning, through his own negligence, Phoebe had been forced to fight off unwanted sexual advances. Though he admired the way she'd dismissed it and tried to put it behind her, he knew damn well the experience had shaken her. The last thing she needed only a few hours later was some macho come-on, and from the very man who was supposed to protect her.

He'd meant only to be charming. He'd told himself he just wanted her to like him. She'd injured his male pride by refusing to consider him as potential husband material.

But before long he'd forgotten completely about any narcissistic plans to feed his ego. He'd enjoyed her company. He'd gotten so caught up in talking with her, sharing his dreams for the show, listening to her ideas, that he'd dismissed the stupid marriage book from his mind.

The kiss had come out of nowhere. When she'd spilled the orange juice, then tried to wipe up the mess, her touch had immediately aroused him to the breaking point—a fact that hadn't escaped her attention, unfortunately. Men were at a disadvantage that way.

The kiss was not a calculated seduction. And her response, he was pretty sure, was not a premeditated attempt to woo him into a matrimonial frame of mind. The desires pulsating between them had been too raw, too genuine, to be anything but pure instinct.

As for her well-timed retreat, he could only admire her for it. She really was trying to discourage him. No woman played *that* hard to get.

For whatever reason, she didn't want to marry him. Though that realization might bruise his ego a bit, deep down—really deep—he felt relieved.

In the future, no matter how much he desired her, he would keep their relationship on a completely professional level. If he needed to tell her anything about the show, he would do it at the studio or on the phone.

Satisfied with his decision, he took a quick shower—a nice cold one—and climbed into bed. But sleep was a long time coming.

THE NEXT TWO DAYS went smoothly—almost too smoothly, Wyatt thought. Phoebe showed up at the studio at precisely six a.m. the morning after their orange-juice kiss, looking tired but well polished and professional. Had she lain awake as he had? he wondered, then immediately put a clamp on that line of thought. He had to forget about that night. He was sure she would.

She wasn't cold to him, but neither was she warm and friendly and animated, as she'd been in her apartment. She did her job quickly and efficiently, the models seemed pleased with her work, and she proved a hit with the rest of his staff.

As soon as the show was over, she came to him and asked for a briefing for the next day. Then, at precisely eleven-fifteen, she left.

Where was she going? He knew it was none of his business. He should be concerned with her work performance, nothing else. She claimed she didn't have another job. What, then? A boyfriend? If she was in a relationship, why hadn't she just told him, instead of pretending she didn't have time for men?

Was the guy someone she was ashamed of? Maybe he was in prison, and she rushed out of the studio so she could make visiting hours.

He had to laugh at his own speculation. Phoebe wasn't dumb enough to date someone in prison, but a boyfriend was the only explanation for her behavior that made sense to him. She was looking for a husband, she'd found a candidate, but she didn't want to share him yet. That was acceptable, he supposed.

Acceptable, hell. It made him inexplicably, inappropriately furious.

After meeting with Kelly and Kurt about a wardrobe problem, Wyatt stepped into his director's office to brainstorm about upcoming shows. One of the things he did as producer was encourage the entire staff, from the director down to the lowliest grip, to contribute ideas. He figured everybody operated in a slightly different sphere. The more spies he had out in the world keeping their eyes and ears open for cutting-edge trends, the less likely he was to miss something important coming down the pike.

His director, Phyllis Cardenza, was a tiny dynamo of a woman who was as dedicated to the show as he was. She was 45, divorced, with two teenagers on whom she doted.

"We've got the dog trainer confirmed for next Wednesday," she said, as soon as Wyatt stepped into her office.

"Great. What about the breeder with that new... what's it called?"

"A thimble poodle. She's confirmed, too."

"Okay, what about..." Wyatt's words trailed off as he spotted a familiar blue-and-white book peeking out from under some papers on Phyllis's desk. He grasped a corner of the book and pulled it out. "Phyllis, I had no idea you were husband-hunting."

"Oh, stop it, it's not for me," she said, grabbing the book back from him. "Haven't you looked at the bestseller list lately? *2001 Ways to Wed* is hot. Number five this week. I'm predicting number one next week."

"You're kidding? Doesn't that strike you as kind of...I don't know. Distasteful?" he asked Phyllis.

"Why?"

"I don't know. The whole idea of a woman plotting to trap a husband seems so archaic." And out of character for Phoebe, he added silently. "Aren't women more liberated these days?"

"It's not that way at all." Phyllis handed the book back to him. "Read it. I've already got a call in to Jane Jasmine's agent—don't look at me like that, I wouldn't book anyone without your okay. I just wanted to see when she might be available. All the single women I know are reading this book, and I even know a couple who swear Jane's advice really works."

Wyatt took the book, his mind suddenly churning with ideas. "Maybe we could get a few people on the show who've found husbands by using the book," he said, thinking aloud.

"Or, maybe we could bring some hopeless cases on—you know, women who think they'll never find a man—and Jane can do a relationship makeover on them, give them some strategies, then bring them back in a few weeks to see how they've done."

"Phyllis, you're brilliant." And it was a great idea, as long as Phyllis didn't get wind that their makeup artist was one of Jane's devotees. Phyllis would probably suggest they put her on as one of Jane's experiments, and men all over the country would know she was available and looking. Wyatt didn't care for that idea at all.

ON THURSDAY, Phoebe got a break. Her late-afternoon economics class got canceled, so she came home, more exhausted than she could ever remember being. She was actually working fewer hours than she did at the spa. But the tension of working so close to Wyatt and pretending she felt nothing for him was wearing her out.

She'd been skipping her swimming workouts, too, which contributed to her crankiness. When she'd been working at Sunrise, she could usually slip in a few laps between clients. Now she had to either swim at night or not at all, and the evenings had been too cool for swimming.

This afternoon, however, it was downright hot, and she was wilted as a week-old rose. A swim in Mesa Blue's meticulously maintained pool sounded like just the thing to revive her body and her spirits. She was doubly glad of her decision when she found Elise and Frannie in the pool, paddling around on rafts.

"Your class got canceled, too?" Elise asked when she spied Phoebe walking across the courtyard in her hot-pink one-piece.

"Yeah, some staff development thing." Phoebe made a clean racer's dive into the pool and swam one lap, but her energy abandoned her at that point, so she sat on the steps at the shallow end and put on her straw hat to protect her face from the sun.

"How's the new job?" Frannie asked anxiously, paddling close to Phoebe.

"It's fine." Phoebe really didn't want to talk about it, but Frannie, meaning well, persisted.

"So what's Wyatt really like?"

The sexiest man alive. "He's okay. A good boss, considerate and respectful. Works hard. His staff really seems to like him, so they work hard for him. He's not an egomaniac like most of the producers I've worked with. He takes a lot of pride in his work, and he's not too proud to—" She stopped herself before she nominated Wyatt for sainthood.

Elise and Frannie listened with rapt expressions, smiling slightly. "He sounds like he really is the paragon his grandparents make him out to be," Elise said.

"He's okay," Phoebe finished lamely.

Elise gave her a knowing look. "You're not telling us something."

"What wouldn't I be telling you?" Phoebe asked, but her studied nonchalance obviously didn't fool Elise.

"Like maybe you have a thing for him? Daisy said he has one for you."

"Daisy's been inhaling too much pottery glaze."

"Methinks the lady doth protest too—"

"I do not!"

Frannie ended the semi-heated discussion by grabbing an arm from both Elise and Phoebe. "Oh, my gosh, Bill's coming. Hide me."

"Hide you?" Elise and Phoebe said together.

"I look too fat in this bathing suit!"

Phoebe gave Frannie a once-over. She wore a one-piece suit with a skirt, and it had pictures of—what else?—cats all over it. "Frannie, you have a very cute figure and you look great in that suit."

"Remember what Jane Jasmine says," Elise reminded Frannie, as Bill came closer, strolling along with his toolbox and whistling tunelessly. "'No matter what size or shape you are, be proud of it.'"

"She's probably a size two!" Frannie groused. But when Bill waved jauntily to the women, Frannie smiled and waved back. "Hi, Bill. Did you get a chance to look at my car?"

"Oh, yeah, Frannie. It was just a loose wire. All fixed."

Frannie batted her eyelashes and pushed her chest out a bit. "I just don't know what I'd do without your help. I'm so hopeless when it comes to anything mechanical."

"My pleasure." Bill tipped his baseball cap, then continued on his way.

"Frannie!" Elise scolded. "Stop playing dumb with him. Men don't fall for that helpless act anymore."

"Oh, rats, I keep forgetting. That's what I did when I was a girl, and old habits are hard to break."

Elise gave Frannie's shoulders a squeeze. "It's okay. I think Bill's pretty smitten no matter what you do."

"But he does like it when I'm more self-sufficient. I changed my own air-conditioning filters the other day, and he was so proud of me I thought his shirt buttons would pop off."

"See?" Phoebe said. "It's the ones who *want* you to be helpless and dumb you have to watch out for."

And she'd encountered plenty of that type. In fact, she seemed to attract that type.

Even Wyatt sometimes talked down to her. He treated her like she had a mind of her own. Oh, he respected her skill, even if she was just a lowly makeup artist. But he over-explained things.

How would he feel, she wondered, if he knew her true career aspirations? What would he think about kissing a future biochemist who planned to manufacture cosmetics instead of put them on other people's faces?

Her fellow students and her professors treated her differently than most people. Though she'd gotten her share of stares her first semester, her study buddies now treated her like an intellectual equal—something new and refreshing for Phoebe. But Wyatt already knew her on a safe, nonthreatening level. Would he go weird on her if he found out she was brainy? Elise had warned her that some men were intimidated by an intelligent woman, and that she ought to be prepared for it.

"Yo, Zombie Woman," Elise said.

Phoebe snapped back to attention. She'd been zoning out.

"You'd better put some sunscreen on."

She swam laps, instead, hoping that if she worked her body hard enough, she would banish her hopeless thoughts regarding Wyatt Madison.

AT 11:10 ON FRIDAY, Wyatt found Phoebe predictably packing up her cosmetics, preparing for her flight.

He leaned in through the doorway. "The whole

crew is heading to Vito's for lunch in a few minutes,''
he said. "It's kind of a tradition, our version of a staff
meeting. I hope you can join us."

She looked up, her regret obvious. "I really wish
I could, but I've got plans."

"You can't rearrange them, just this once?" he
prodded.

She shook her head. "Maybe next Friday I can.
Now that I know it's important. My schedule isn't
very flexible, but with some advance notice I can usually manage."

"Oh, that reminds me," Wyatt said. "Kelly has to
take next Friday off, so we're taping Friday's show
on Wednesday afternoon. Is that a problem?"

Phoebe looked almost stricken. "All afternoon?"

"We'll probably be done by three. But then you
can take Friday off."

"You might want to look around for a substitute
makeup artist," she said. "I'll see what I can arrange
and let you know Monday, but afternoons are a problem."

"What keeps you so busy in the afternoon?" he
asked, keeping his tone light and playful. "Hot
date?"

She smiled. "Nothing like that." She glanced at
her watch. "I really have to go. Sorry I can't join the
group for lunch."

"That's okay. I'll brief you later. I did promise
when I hired you that the hours were regular, so I
guess I can't renege on that now."

"I appreciate that." She closed and locked her
case, picked it up as if it were nothing—and he knew
it weighed a ton—and brushed past him out of the

dressing room. His body immediately reacted to her nearness, her fresh floral scent, but she seemed oblivious. "'Bye, have a nice weekend."

That sounded as if she didn't plan on seeing or talking to him until Monday, which irritated him no end. Where did she run off to every day? The mystery was driving him crazy.

Impulsively, he raced to Phyllis's office and stuck his head in the door. "I can't come to Vito's today."

She looked surprised. He ducked out before she could voice an objection, then headed for the parking lot. He reached the exit just in time to see Phoebe climbing into a cute compact car.

He knew he was acting nuts, but he couldn't help it. He ducked behind a row of cars so she wouldn't see him, then tucked and ran to his own car and jumped in. He started it up and backed out, waited until he saw which direction Phoebe headed, then followed.

He tailed her for twenty minutes. She was heading out of town, through the suburb of Tempe. His imagination ran wild. Maybe she had a secret double life: a husband and kids somewhere who thought she spent all her time visiting a sick grandmother in Phoenix. Maybe she was an exotic dancer in some out-of-the-way club. Maybe she was visiting a drug treatment center, kicking a coke habit.

Or maybe— His appalling speculations came to a screeching halt when Phoebe's car turned into the main entrance of the Arizona State University campus. She was visiting a college? What on earth for? Was she selling Avon products to co-eds, maybe cutting and styling hair in the dorms for extra money?

She'd said she didn't have another job, but maybe she was afraid Wyatt would want her to work exclusively for his show if he found out about her extracurricular activities.

He followed her, as she wove her way down this drive and that, finally parking in a lot that required a blue sticker, which her car seemed to have. So this was someplace she belonged.

Since he didn't have a parking permit, he pulled his Jag under a tree in a No Parking zone. He would only be here a minute, he reasoned. He watched as Phoebe climbed out of her car, lugging what looked like a heavy backpack, and headed for the entrance of the nearest building, which was the library.

A tall, thin young man with thick glasses greeted her on the library steps. She gave him a quick hug— more a shoulder squeeze, really—then they both sat down on the steps. He had a backpack, too—which seemed to be standard issue on this campus; every kid who walked past had one. He opened his pack and pulled out two paper-wrapped items, then handed one to her. It was a sandwich. The two of them chatted and ate lunch. Phoebe opened her pack, pulled out two bottles of something, and handed one to the kid.

So, Wyatt thought, supremely disappointed, his first instinct had been right. Phoebe had a boyfriend, some possibly underage kid she wanted to keep secret. From what he knew about Phoebe, her choice didn't make much sense. She was a TV star, a completely gorgeous woman who could probably attract any guy in the world just by crooking her little finger. He didn't even eliminate himself; if she even half tried, she could have him. She'd bent him completely out of shape with no effort at all.

So why was she involved with some zit-faced kid who hadn't even finished school?

"Wait a minute..." He leaned back between the seats until he found what he was looking for—the copy of *2001 Ways to Wed* Phyllis had loaned him. He hadn't done much more than scan through it, but even so he'd been impressed with the common-sense, down-to-earth advice Ms. Jasmine gave her readers. She appeared to understand how men's thought processes worked. Although she wasn't above using a trick or two to *meet* men, she was against using any kind of subterfuge once a woman had a man's attention. Instead of advising women to trick men into marriage, she encouraged her readers to simply understand what men wanted.

He flipped through the book again, finally locating the chapter he thought he remembered seeing: "Lessons in Love: Get an Education." Most worthwhile men, Jane advised, liked a woman who could think. By pursuing educational avenues that interested her, whether it was history or computer science, a woman could double her chances of meeting the right man. First, she was improving herself, and second, she was expanding her base of friends and acquaintances.

Apparently Phoebe had taken Jane's advice to heart. He wondered what kind of class she might be taking. He didn't think Arizona State offered cosmetology classes, but he could be wrong. Maybe PE, he speculated. Something was keeping her body in unbelievable condition.

When he saw a campus police car headed his way,

he put his Jag in gear and pulled away. He'd seen enough. If she was trolling college campuses for a husband, it was none of his business. He would simply put it out of his mind. He wouldn't think about Phoebe again until he saw her Monday morning.

But he found he couldn't dismiss her from his thoughts so easily. What was she thinking? If she was intent on robbing the cradle, at least she could pick a good-looking, studly student, one who would measure up to her in the looks department.

Obviously Phoebe needed some relationship advice. He was older and wiser than she; he'd been in relationships good and bad, he'd seen friends fall in love, get married, get divorced. He could give her some much-needed guidance, before she did something stupid like marry some totally inappropriate guy just because she craved a white picket fence.

Besides, it was in his best interest to keep her happy and well grounded. She was his employee. He depended on her to show up every day, focused and ready to work. So far she'd done that, but who knew what would happen next week if Joe College threw her over? He felt suddenly quite paternal toward Phoebe, very protective. Though it might not be pleasant, he was obligated to sit her down and talk sense into her. Tonight, if possible.

PHOEBE HAD NEVER BEEN so happy to see the weekend. Three mid-term exams in one week was hellish; five straight days of working with Wyatt had been more than enough to fray her nerves.

Tonight, she thought as she pulled into the Mesa

Blue parking lot, she would order a pizza, put on her jammies, climb into bed and watch old movies....

The sight of Wyatt's Jag in its spot distracted her for a moment, but then she chastised herself for letting such a little thing bother her. The man did live here, at least temporarily. He had a right to relax at home on the weekend. Anyway, what were the chances she would run into him? The whole first week he'd lived at Mesa Blue she'd hardly glimpsed him.

Her optimism was dashed as she stopped in the elegant lobby to collect her mail. She said hello to the security guard, put her key into her mailbox, then sensed a presence approaching from behind—the unmistakable aura of Wyatt Madison.

"Hey, Phoebe."

He sounded pretty cheerful. She guessed that meant he wasn't as hot and bothered around her as she was around him. She glanced over at him. He was still in his work clothes, apparently just getting home from the station. He had a plastic grocery sack, which he'd set down by his feet.

"Hello, Wyatt. How's your house-hunting going?"

"Haven't had much time for looking, but I'm supposed to go out with the real estate agent tomorrow."

He didn't sound too enthused. "Did you talk to Elise about buying her unit?" she asked, then wanted to bite her tongue. All she needed was for Wyatt to move into Mesa Blue permanently. Having him living next door for a few weeks was making her tense enough.

"I did, but she won't be ready to sell until the fall. My grandparents love me, but I don't think they'll want me underfoot for that long. Oh, look, here's a postcard from them. Greece.''

"I have one, too!" Phoebe announced, holding up the colorful card of Athens. "How sweet of them to think of me." She turned it over and read aloud: "'Dear Phoebe, we're having a wonderful time. I hope you and Wyatt are getting along. Please remind him to water the plants on the balcony and talk to the cactus. Love, Rolland and Helen.'" She turned to him. "Wyatt, water the plants on the balcony and talk to the cactus."

He laughed, then read his card. "Mine says, 'Dearest Wyatt, we're having a wonderful time. If you're having any problems settling in, please ask Phoebe. She knows everything. Don't forget to water the plants and talk to the cactus—'"

"What's the deal with the cactus?" Phoebe asked. "I know Helen loves her plants, but I never heard her talk to them before."

"She bought some new ones just before the trip, a couple of cacti. The lady who sold them to her said they would bloom if she talked nice to them."

Phoebe laughed. "I'm sorry I interrupted. What else does the card say?"

"That's it, just 'Love, Grammy and Granddad.'"

"You call Helen 'Grammy'?" She couldn't suppress a chuckle at the thought of big, macho Wyatt calling *anybody* "Grammy."

"What's wrong with that? What do you call your grandmother?"

Phoebe sighed. "I never knew either of them. One lived in Denmark, so I never met her. The other I didn't see after my parents split up when I was a baby. But she remembered me. She left me her condo when she died.''

''I'm sorry. I forgot for a minute that you'd lost your grandmother. I shouldn't have been so glib.''

Phoebe shrugged, wishing she'd never brought up the subject of grandmothers. She'd always regretted that she hadn't made an effort to see her father's mother before the woman died. Her grandmother had sent an occasional letter, and usually a card with a few dollars tucked inside on Phoebe's birthday, and Phoebe had dutifully sent thank-you notes, but her mother hadn't encouraged communication even though her grandmother had obviously wanted it. Olga's bitterness toward her ex-husband colored her thinking.

Still, Phoebe had no business unloading any personal stuff onto Wyatt.

And he didn't have to be so damn sympathetic. It just made her like him more, and she didn't need any more reasons to be attracted to him. Wrong time, wrong man, she reminded herself.

''How was lunch?'' she asked brightly, changing the subject.

He didn't answer right away.

''Was it that hard a question?'' As she sorted through her bills, she peeked at him from the corner of her eye. He really did seem to be having trouble answering.

''Lunch was fine,'' he said carefully. ''But some things did come up, and I need to talk to you about them.''

Uh-oh. ''You're not pleased with my job performance?''

"No, oh, you're doing a great job, Phoebe. You have a real talent for making people look their best on camera."

"Thanks."

"But I do need to talk to you."

"Now?"

"I know it's been a long week, but I want to…go over a few things while they're fresh in my mind. It won't take long, I promise." He reached into the plastic bag at his feet, pulled out a package of something, then shook it invitingly at her. "Gourmet coffee?"

Sure enough, it was a half-pound of Jamaican Blue Mountain, her favorite kind. She could smell it.

"I thought you didn't drink coffee."

"I don't, but I got some to have on hand for guests."

For sleep-over guests, she added. A non-coffee-drinker didn't spring for Jamaican Blue Mountain unless he was trying to impress someone. Could that someone possibly be her?

Chapter Seven

Her old movies could wait, Phoebe decided. Though on principle she didn't like employers to monopolize her free time, Wyatt was paying her a ridiculously high salary for part-time work, so she couldn't begrudge him an occasional after-hours meeting. After all, she *had* skipped the staff lunch meeting today.

"I'll be over in a few minutes," she said, feeling a small surge of energy mixed with something akin to dread. It wasn't that she didn't like Wyatt. She did, probably too much. The idea that he'd bought that coffee for *her*...well, it was just nice, that was all, and it made her want to please him.

But he made her tense. Since that kiss, the desire had crackled between them whenever they were within twenty feet of each other. She would have to let that go, she decided. Surely it was simply a matter of their getting more accustomed to each other.

Phoebe changed into comfortable clothes, filed her mail and listened to her phone messages. She wasn't too surprised to get a panicky-sounding message from her mother. Olga considered it a major crisis if she broke a nail, and she called Phoebe almost every day in a tizzy over something or other.

"Addy, call me right away!" Olga said breathlessly. She never called Phoebe by her "Hollywood" name, even though Olga was the one who'd encouraged Adelaide Phelps to morph into Phoebe Lane. "I *have* to talk to you."

Phoebe shook her head and rewound the tape. She would call Olga back once she got done with Wyatt.

When she stepped out her front door a few minutes later, the coffee was already brewing at Wyatt's. She could smell it all the way down the hall, and it drew her in like a siren song.

Wyatt let her in, and she immediately took note of his own casual attire—jeans faded almost to white and another T-shirt. Had she actually tried to tell herself she didn't like those clothes on him? He looked so approachable. Huggable. She almost wished for another broken pipe so she could see that T-shirt clinging to every muscle—

No. She was going to learn to enjoy him and appreciate him as a friend, neighbor and co-worker. Nothing more.

"The coffee's almost ready," he said by way of greeting. "We can sit out on the balcony if you want."

She nodded. "Yes, that sounds nice."

He poured her a mug of the fragrant brew, himself a glass of skim milk—was he a health nut?—and wandered out to the terrace, which looked like nothing so much as a rain forest with all the fronds and vines. All appeared to be thriving.

"Looks like these plants aren't suffering under your care," she observed.

"I water them first thing every morning."

"These cactus plants aren't blooming." She leveled a frown of disapproval at him. "Are you talking to them?"

"Of course. I'm not taking any chances. I sweet-talk them twice a day—or face being disowned."

"I seriously doubt Rolland or Helen would disown you. They think you walk on water and carry stardust in your pockets."

Wyatt laughed, as they found chairs, a nice, safe distance apart. "If I've turned out well at all, it's their doing. I was not exactly your basic well-behaved, well-adjusted boy."

"I'd never guess that. According to them, you were a perfect child."

"They must have a lot of suppressed memories."

Enough, Phoebe thought. This conversation was too personal, too intimate. She set her coffee on the glass-top table, opened her notebook, took a pen from the bib pocket of her overalls, and prepared to be a good little employee.

"So what went on at the staff meeting?" she asked brightly.

Again, that hesitation from Wyatt.

"I ended up not going to Vito's for lunch," he finally said. "Instead, I followed you."

Phoebe suddenly felt as if she couldn't gulp in enough breath. She was not going to fly off the handle, she coached herself. Wyatt must have a logical reason for following her. "W-Why?" she managed to stutter.

"I was worried about you. I know it's not my place to be your watchdog—"

"It certainly isn't," she couldn't help saying.

"But after what happened on Monday—"

"Please, can we forget about that?"

"It just occurred to me that you're very vulnerable. A woman living alone, and not just any woman but a TV star—"

"Used-to-be TV star."

"Still, you make an easy target for any wacko nutcase who's seen 'Skin Deep.'"

"So you're planning to follow me around for the rest of my life to make sure no one makes a pass at me?"

"No! It's just that, the way you rush away from the station each day, obviously with someplace to go, and the fact that you're so mysterious about it—"

"It's my private life!" It was all she could do to keep her voice low enough that all of Mesa Blue wouldn't hear her.

"I know, and I apologize, but I started worrying that you'd gotten involved in something bad, maybe something you couldn't handle—"

"Well, if you followed me, you know the horrible truth now," she said, feeling almost violated. Going to college was nothing to be ashamed of. She knew that. But it was part of her dream for the future, and after seeing other high-flown, much-bandied-about dreams shattered, she now preferred to keep hers very private.

"Is he going to marry you?" Wyatt asked quietly.

"What?" Had she missed some vital part of the conversation? "Who?"

"The guy. On the library steps?"

Phoebe almost laughed out loud. "You mean Richie?"

"Yeah, Richie—whatever. Isn't that what we're talking about?"

"Not that I knew of."

"Look, I know it's none of my business—"

"Damn straight." Too restless to continue sitting, she jumped up and paced to the balcony railing.

"—but if you're determined to get married, surely you can find a better prospect than a beanpole college kid barely old enough to shave."

Try as she might, Phoebe couldn't make sense of what Wyatt was saying. "Where did you get the notion I wanted to get married? That is the *last* thing I want or need right now."

He joined her at the railing, making her wish she'd stayed in her nice, safe chair. She couldn't think straight with him so close, smelling so good. Even the way he breathed was sexy.

"I know it says in that book that you shouldn't broadcast your intentions," he said, almost gently, "that it makes you look desperate, but—"

"What—" she started to ask, but then realized she knew exactly what book. While she'd been changing clothes last Monday night, he'd been snooping on her bookshelf.

"*2001 Ways to Wed,*" he said, confirming her suspicions. "Don't bother denying you've read it, I saw it in your apartment, and I saw you'd made notes in the margins."

She was stunned, insulted, and maybe a little relieved, at the way he'd constructed an alternative reality from the little bits of information he'd gathered from her life.

"How dare you presume..." But she stopped there and changed tack. "Guess there's just no fooling you, Wyatt Madison." What else could she say? If she told him the book was for Daisy's sake, not hers, she would be violating Daisy's privacy.

Anyway, it was safer if he thought she was husband-hunting. For one, he'd definitely give her a wide berth. No confirmed bachelor wanted to be trapped or manipulated into walking down the aisle.

"I know Jane Jasmine recommends taking classes to meet the man of your dreams," he said, "but I don't think she meant for someone your age and, er, maturity level to set her sights on, well, someone like this Richie."

"What's wrong with Richie?" she couldn't resist asking.

"He's too young for you!" Wyatt exploded. "Does he have a job? Hell, he probably lives with his parents, or in a dorm!"

"He has an apartment, I think, and he's an engineering major, which means he'll have a high-paying job the moment he graduates. But what does that matter? I would never marry a guy just because he has a good job."

"Then what *do* you see in him?"

Phoebe knew she should tell Wyatt the truth. Richie was a study buddy. Actually, she tutored *him.* Instead of paying her, he brought her lunch every day, giving her a few extra precious minutes to decompress from work. But again, it was easier if she let Wyatt assume what he wanted to.

"Richie is very sweet," she said.

"I'm sure he is, but Lord, Phoebe, you can do better. Are you sleeping with him?"

"You know, Wyatt," she said, finding this conversation less and less humorous, "you're sounding an awful lot like you're jealous."

The stunned look on his face was almost comical. "No! I just don't want to see you ruin your life by jumping into marriage with...with..." He sagged a bit. "Hell, yes, I'm jealous," he muttered. "If you want a husband so bad, why was I never even in the running?"

Phoebe's heart just about stopped beating. She'd only been trying to get a rise out of him. She hadn't imagined he really *was* jealous. His honesty, his willingness to make himself vulnerable, touched her as nothing else could. It was time to stop playing games.

"You were in the running," she said. "A top candidate for a while."

He looked at her, surprised. "And you ruled me out because..."

"Because Daisy said you weren't right for her."

WYATT JUST STARED at her as the puzzle pieces clicked into place—in the right order, this time. She was helping Daisy find a husband. Duh. Hadn't she been trying to set him up with Daisy the night of Elise's engagement party?

Now, because he'd misunderstood, because he was so damn competitive, and because he'd had a bruised ego the size of Arizona, he'd all but asked Phoebe to marry him. Their hands almost touched where they rested near each other on the balcony railing, and she looked at him with those luminous blue eyes, as if she expected something.

What had he done? How was he going to escape the trap he'd set and thrown himself into?

But suddenly he didn't want to escape. He wanted to be enfolded in Phoebe's slender arms. He wanted to kiss her incredible mouth and drink in the taste of her, the scent of her that he could never quite get out of his mind. He wanted her long blond hair to spill over him the way it had the other night, like spun white-gold silk.

"So you're not marrying Richie?" he asked in a hoarse voice, just to be sure he really understood.

"I'm not marrying anybody, including you." It sounded like a promise, a solemn vow, the way she said it. Her eyes held a certain sadness. But they also held invitation.

He could think of a million reasons why he shouldn't kiss her, and only one reason he should. He wanted her like he'd never wanted a woman in his life. All the reasons he should send her home melted away in the face of his growing passion. With great deliberation he reached for her. With a little gasp of surprise she took a step back—into one of the cactus plants. She yelped and sprang forward right into his arms.

Right where he wanted her.

"Are you okay?" he asked, holding her gently so she could get away if she wanted to.

Apparently she didn't, because she tolerated his light embrace.

"Darn cactus."

"Good cactus," he crooned, sifting a handful of

her incredible hair through his fingers. Then he bent down to claim what was his. His for the moment, anyway.

She didn't resist. If he'd felt even a tiny hesitation he'd have stopped, refusing to be just another Taylor Shad in her life. But she moved eagerly into his embrace, winding her arms around his neck, burying her fingers in his hair. He could feel her warm breath on his cheek and taste the coffee she'd just drunk. It was enough to make him want to start drinking the stuff.

"Wyatt," she whispered, breaking the kiss and breathing heavily.

He felt her soft breasts rising and falling against his chest. It would be so easy to slide one hand inside the loose overalls.

"Please..." she almost moaned.

He stopped his gentle assault on her neck, falling completely still. He must be crazy to come on so strong. He was acting like an animal.

"I'll stop," he said, though it cost him. He focused his mind on brussels sprouts and visualized burying himself in ice cubes.

"No. I mean, don't stop." She kissed him again, desperately, greedily.

He buried his face in her hair. "I hope you're not relying on my self-control to stop this, because I just used up the last of it."

"Make love to me, Wyatt."

He was a little surprised by the directness of the request but not stupid enough to turn her down. "You're sure? This has nothing to do with the fact that I sign your paycheck?"

"Are you trying to talk me out of it?"

Her eyes had gone all heavy-lidded and dreamy. She licked her lips, which just about did him in, then started to kiss him again.

"Not out here." He took her hand—it felt small and sweet and helpless—and led her inside. The moment he closed the door and the curtain, she was kissing him again. He could hardly believe what a bundle of passion she'd become, once unleashed. Especially after a week's worth of her tightly reserved demeanor at work. But he wasn't going to question it.

"Are you protected?" he asked, amazed he had that much presence of mind.

She gave a little gasp. "No. Please tell me you have something here."

"Somewhere." He hoped. He hadn't entertained any overnight guests since moving to Phoenix. "We'll work it out." Impatient now, he scooped her into his arms and kissed her while he walked her into the guest bedroom where he'd set up camp.

He didn't turn on any lights, feeling his way blindly through the room. When his shin hit the double bed, he stopped and put her down.

"This isn't your grandparents' room, is it?" she asked apprehensively.

He chuckled. "No. I don't think I'd be able to make whoopee in Grammy and Grandpa's bed. Too weird. Don't go anywhere."

He searched through his chest of drawers, going by feel. He'd seen some condoms around here somewhere. Sock drawer, maybe? Or in that drawer where he'd stashed all those suspenders and cuff links he never wore?

"Why don't you turn on a light?" Phoebe suggested, sounding anxious.

"Because I like the dark." He tried to be mysterious. The truth was, he didn't want to chance destroying the mood. His body was primed to make love with Phoebe Lane, and if she came to her senses now, he would have to jump off his balcony and end it all.

Besides, he didn't want her to see what a mess his bedroom was. He wasn't the world's best housekeeper. If he'd had any idea what the evening might have led to, he'd have straightened up a little.

"Any luck?" she asked.

"Yes, I think—no, damn it, it's a sample packet of aspirin. Do you have any…?"

"No." Pure despair. "Maybe Elise has some. Oh, my God, what am I thinking? I can't ask Elise for *that*. We'll just have to go to the store. Or maybe…"

Don't say it, he silently pleaded. *Don't say we should give up and call it quits.*

He heard her moving, heard the bed springs squeak. She found him in the dark, where he stood just inside the closet door, feeling around on the top shelf. She put her arms around his middle.

"Come to bed, Wyatt," she said, the words a sexy caress. "You're a creative problem-solver. I'm sure together we can figure something out."

He was already hard as granite inside his jeans. Her implied suggestion caused him to almost lose his cool completely, especially when her hand sort of accidentally-on-purpose brushed against his fly.

Just then his fingers closed around a familiar-feeling plastic packet. Just one, but that would do for now. "Eureka," he said as he pressed the packet into her hand.

They didn't waste any more time. Wyatt managed to shed his clothes in the four steps it took him to get from the closet to the bed. He shucked Phoebe out of her overalls the way he might peel a banana, now wishing he'd turned on a light so he could see her.

"What color are your panties?" he asked as he slid them down her incredibly long legs.

"Wyatt!"

"I have to know."

"I don't remember! Probably white. I have boring underwear."

"Impossible, not when you're in it." He pulled her T-shirt over her head, then cupped her full breasts in his hands.

"You can't tell me this bra is anything but boring," she argued. "It's for jogging. Flattens me out."

"We can't have that." With a flick of his hand he undid the clasp in back.

She tossed the offending garment aside, and all teasing stopped there. She was a goddess with velvet skin and hands that worked magic wherever they brushed against him. He tore back the covers on his bed and fell onto it, pulling her with him. She covered him chest to toe, the exquisite contact making him groan.

He didn't want to rush her, but he was walking a tightrope. "Where's the—"

"I've got it."

"Can you—"

"Yes."

And she did. Wyatt bit his lip against the white-hot pleasure of Phoebe's hands touching him so intimately. Those sweet, helpless hands weren't so helpless, after all.

"Are you—"

"Uh-huh."

"Do you want—"

"No, it's perfect like this."

He could get used to her reading his mind.

She straddled him, poising herself over him and hesitating just long enough that he thought he might have to beg. Then she sheathed him with excruciating slowness, accommodating herself to him inch by agonizing inch.

She gave a gusty sigh when he was buried deeply inside her.

"Is everything okay?" he whispered. He would commit *hara-kiri* before he would hurt her.

"Yes. Oh, yes. It's been a while, that's all."

He was relieved to hear that. "For me, too. I won't last long."

"Me, neither."

Amazingly, though, he did. Because she was on top, Phoebe pretty much set the pace, but she managed to keep him on the edge of a nuclear explosion for a good long while, speeding up, then slowing down almost to a standstill, trembling slightly, then starting the whole process over again. Still, there came a point when he couldn't take it anymore. He grasped her hips and thrust inside her, quickly, deeply, and with one final groan of pure ecstasy he let go.

When sanity returned, Phoebe was collapsed against him, her hair covering them both in a silken waterfall, just as it had in his fantasy. It occurred to him then what a totally selfish bastard he was. He'd completely neglected her pleasure.

"Phoebe?"

"Hmm."

"Tell me what to do."

"Shut up and enjoy the afterglow. It's my favorite part."

"But you didn't…"

She raised herself up and looked at him, amused. "Only about three times." She shrugged. "I'm not very showy."

He laughed out loud and hugged her against him, relieved. How had he ever been fortunate enough to end up in bed with Phoebe Lane? She was one in a million.

But the feeling of euphoria quickly faded. What, exactly, did he want from Phoebe? Why had he taken her to bed now, as opposed to last week or next week? Granted, she'd been the one to initiate physical closeness, but he could have backed off.

Probably should have, he reflected. Maybe she was on the level about this husband-hunting thing. Maybe she didn't want a permanent attachment at this point in her life. But she definitely wanted something. He'd never met a woman yet who made love to a man without any expectations.

He couldn't offer her much. Intellectually, he'd known taking her to bed wasn't fair or wise or circumspect. He had to work with this woman every day, and for good or bad, what they'd done here tonight would have an effect on their professional relationship. He wasn't dumb enough to believe it wouldn't.

So why had he done it? It wasn't simple lack of self-control. He'd made a conscious decision to make love to her.

Was it a macho thing? The thought of all those college studs vying for her attention—and possibly getting it—made him want to claim her, brand her, mark her as his territory, put a No Trespassing sign on her. Every man who saw her wanted her, but Wyatt Madison had gotten her. Was that it? An ego trip?

She sighed in her sleep, and his heart softened. He stroked her hair, letting the fine strands sift through his fingers. He shouldn't be so hard on himself. How could he have resisted her allure, even if he'd wanted to?

They weren't right for each other, he knew that. He was too old for her, for one thing. She would be wanting to start a family in the next few years. He'd pretty much written off that idea for himself. Him, with a baby? Pretty ludicrous.

But tonight they'd been too lonely people who'd found each other. They'd behaved responsibly. And for a few hours, they'd each been a little less lonely. He hadn't made any promises or given her any reason to expect more than he could give.

Maybe they would make love again, or maybe they wouldn't. But there was no reason to let one slightly rash decision ruin their friendship.

But even as he turned the possibilities over in his mind, he knew he would have to be careful. There was something about Phoebe that made him want to open up, to share things he'd never shared with anyone. He felt this tremendous urge to pull his heart right out of his chest and hand it over, to put it right into those pretty, not-so-helpless hands of hers.

On that path lay trouble.

Phoebe's body relaxed into sleep, still lying partially on top of him. He shifted her gently to the side. Her even breathing didn't break. A sound sleeper, then.

He slipped out of bed, and without turning on a light he straightened up the room, putting all his dirty clothes in the bathroom hamper, laying hers neatly over the back of a chair. When Phoebe woke up tomorrow and saw this room for the first time, she might experience some morning-after regrets, but at least she wouldn't think she'd gone to bed with a slob.

Maybe he'd make her French toast in the morning.

PHOEBE AWOKE in the dark, disoriented for a few minutes until she realized where she was. The memory of her lovemaking with Wyatt put an immediate smile on her face. Wow. She'd never experienced anything quite like that before.

It wasn't just the physical aspects of lovemaking, which were admittedly spectacular. It was everything else—his concern about coming on too strong, the fact that he'd thought about protecting her, his frantic search for a condom, his determination that she enjoy the experience as much as he did.

She'd felt comfortable with him, without the usual self-doubts, without that troublesome ''icky'' feeling she'd gotten in the past when she'd made love to

someone she shouldn't have. Everything had felt...
right.

He stirred beside her, throwing a possessive arm
over her, but he didn't wake. She snuggled deeper
into the covers and sighed. She'd meant it when she
told him she enjoyed afterglow even more than the
sex act itself. For her, it was a warm sense of oneness
with her partner, with the whole world.

Unfortunately, it didn't last forever. Harsh reality
returned, and in this case it was harsher than usual.

She'd gone to bed with her boss.

In L.A. she'd spent a lot of time and energy ra-
tionalizing the fact she was sleeping with her producer, hoping futilely she hadn't deep-sixed her acting career. Sleeping with Joel hadn't been the
career-buster, though. Breaking up with him had.

Was her situation any less dire with Wyatt? At least
she could feel pretty confident Wyatt wouldn't spread
smut about her. She couldn't see him using their intimacy against her. He just wasn't the harassing type.

But she felt she'd somehow betrayed Rolland and
Helen. They'd said to ''be nice'' to Wyatt, and they
obviously had some sort of romantic match in mind
between her and their grandson, but she didn't imagine they'd approve of a one-night stand.

One night.

It was obvious that was all she'd get. Wyatt had
been pretty clear he didn't want any attachments.
There was a reason he was a confirmed bachelor at
thirty-nine. Her confidence bolstered by a sudden
burst of need, she'd come on pretty strong, and he'd
responded. She couldn't blame him for anything.

Herself, she could blame. Loneliness was no excuse for throwing herself at a man. Just look what that sort of behavior had done for her mother—a string of men who never stuck around, and zero self-worth.

There were worse things than being without a man, she told herself, as she had so often told Olga. She'd known when she'd set her lofty career goals that she would be making some sacrifices. One of them was forgoing love, marriage and family, at least for a while. Just because this temporary intimacy with Wyatt made her realize what she was missing was no reason to second-guess herself or change her plans.

She had to get out of here. She didn't think she could bear what came with the harsh morning light. Apologies, awkward escapes into the bathroom, halting goodbyes, insincere promises. She would rather keep memories of their night together untainted by such unpleasantness.

She slipped out of bed. Unlike Wyatt, she couldn't move around his bedroom in total darkness, so she opened the door onto the hallway and turned on the bathroom light. The ambient glow was just enough that she could locate her clothes...neatly folded over the back of a chair.

Now, she was sure that wasn't how she'd left them.

With a shrug, she dressed. Wyatt didn't even stir.

She couldn't just leave without a word, she decided. Though he would no doubt be grateful he didn't have to deal with an awkward morning after, it seemed cold to just leave without acknowledging how great last night had been, even if it was a mistake.

He had a small desk in one corner of the bedroom.

In the dim light she rummaged around until she found a pen and a scrap of paper.

After thinking a few moments, she scribbled a few breezy words. He would know she was okay with what had happened and that she expected nothing. That should put his mind at ease.

She placed the note on her pillow, watched him sleep for a few more minutes, then slipped out.

Chapter Eight

Wyatt awoke feeling incredibly well-rested. He hadn't slept that soundly, or that long, in months. Sun streamed through the window, a novelty for him, given that he usually was out of bed before dawn.

Then he remembered the reason for his sense of well-being. In a word, Phoebe.

He reached out to her but encountered nothing but empty space where she ought to be.

Coming more fully awake, he sat up in bed and rubbed his eyes. But that didn't help. The bed was still empty beside him.

"Phoebe?" he called out.

No answer.

Then he saw the note. Hell. A note was bad news. A note meant he'd been kissed off. Unless she'd run out to get bagels or something—but he didn't hold his breath.

He forced himself to read the damn note:

Dear Wyatt:
Thanks for a wonderful evening. I have an early

morning appointment, so I let myself out. See you Monday.

Phoebe

Hell. An *early appointment?* Doing what? With whom? In a fit of unreasoning anger, Wyatt tore up the note. Immediately regretting his fit of pique, he found the bit of paper that had Phoebe's name on it and clenched it in his fist. This was the only tangible evidence that she'd been here.

A note. A damn note.

He ought to be grateful, he thought as he dragged himself out of bed. He'd been wondering what came next, and she answered that question for him. Nothing. Their lovemaking had obviously had little impact on her. She expected them to just go about their lives as they had before.

Wasn't that what he wanted, too? Of course it was. No complications, no recriminations, no clinging female reading unintended meaning into every word, every gesture.

But, damn it, he'd wanted to make French toast for her.

PHOEBE SAT on her balcony, sipping coffee and reading the paper. Some appointment. But she'd thought it would sound nicer if she had an excuse for leaving in the middle of the night. Better if it didn't look like she was running scared.

And she was, she realized. She was downright terrified by what she'd done. She'd broken one of her unbreakable rules by sleeping with her boss. It might

have felt right at the time, but now the regrets just
piled one on top of the other.

What if they found it too uncomfortable to work
together anymore? What if Rolland and Helen found
out? She'd never be able to look them in the eye
again. The warm, familial relationship they'd developed over the years would disintegrate. The Madisons
might love her, but their first loyalty was to Wyatt,
and they wouldn't be quick to forgive her if they perceived that she'd slighted him in any way.

She was grateful for only one thing. Since Wyatt
had gone off on the tangent of believing she was
spending her days at the university looking for potential husbands, he never got around to asking her the
real reason she'd been at ASU.

Maybe he wouldn't.

The phone interrupted her grim musings. She'd left
the balcony door open to bring some fresh air into
her apartment, so all she had to do was step inside to
grab the receiver. The thought briefly crossed her
mind that Wyatt might be calling her, and a silly gid-
diness gripped her heart—until she realized it was her
mother on the line.

"Addy. You didn't call me back," Olga Phelps
said in her odd accent, which held Danish overtones
generously imbued with the results of thirty years of
living in New Jersey.

"Oh, Mama, I'm sorry. I got in too late last night
to call, then this morning I completely—"

"Did you have a date?" Olga asked breathlessly,
Phoebe's transgression forgotten.

Phoebe decided it wouldn't hurt to tell Olga the
truth, or at least some portion of it. She would never

meet Wyatt, and her fondest wish was for her daughter to meet and marry a nice man—since the movie star thing hadn't worked out.

"I got together with a neighbor," Phoebe said, sounding deliberately cagey.

"Who? What neighbor?"

"Wyatt Madison. You know, I've told you about Rolland and Helen Madison?"

"The nice older couple."

"Right. Wyatt's their grandson."

"How old is he?" Olga immediately asked.

"Oh, about thirty-eight or thirty-nine, I think."

Phoebe thought her mother would declare that was too old, and then Phoebe could reassure her that nothing was going to come of their "date." But Olga surprised her.

"That's perfect. Old enough to be settled, and to know how to treat a lady. What does he do?"

Phoebe didn't dare tell her. If her mother discovered Phoebe knew a TV producer, Olga's dreams for Phoebe's show business career would revive in a heartbeat. "He works in, um, public relations," she said, which was almost true. Certainly he dealt with the public.

"And the date went well?" Olga asked, the question dripping with insinuation.

"He's very nice, but I don't think we'll be seeing each other socially anymore. He's a workaholic, and my life is pretty full—"

"Oh, that reminds me why I called in the first place. Adelaide Phelps, how could you keep your new job a secret from your own mother?"

Phoebe cringed. She'd been hoping she could in-

definitely postpone telling Olga about "Heads Up."
Now Olga would be after Phoebe to get herself back
into the limelight, to use this window of opportunity
to revive her dead acting career. She'd always viewed
Phoebe's move to Phoenix and her job at the spa as
a stopgap measure, a brief respite until she landed
another TV or movie role.

"How did you…?" Phoebe began.

"I was watching 'Heads Up,' and I saw your name
in the credits. How long have you been doing that?"

"Just a few days. It was only temporary at first—
I didn't think it was worth mentioning. But now I've
got the job permanently. I was going to tell you about
it." *In five or six years.*

"So what's it like? Do you get to meet movie stars?"

"So far, just Taylor Shad, and it wasn't very pleasant." She shuddered at *that* memory.

"Do you have much sway with the producer?"

Now there was a loaded question, Phoebe thought.

"Could you get booked onto the show as a guest?"
Olga went on, more and more excited. "You are a
TV star, after all."

"'Heads Up' is about trends. They book hot people, not has-been actresses from third-rate TV pro-
grams. Anyway, I'm not interested. I just want to do
makeup."

"That's a real ambitious career you got there."

Phoebe sighed. They'd been through this argument
before. She had once told her mother about going to
college, but Olga had laughed at Phoebe's lofty career
plans. "Addy, honey, you're whistling into the
wind," she'd said. "No one born with your face and
body should waste it on bio-whatever." So Phoebe

hadn't mentioned it again, and she wouldn't, not until she had the diploma in her hand. Maybe not until she'd started her company and had a product on the market with her name on it, something Olga could show to her friends. Now *that* Olga would understand.

"If you don't want to be on the show," Olga said, "that's your choice. But what about me? Could you get me on 'Heads Up'?"

Now it was Phoebe's turn to laugh. "Mama, the show is about cutting-edge trends. What could you possibly do that would qualify?"

"Well, I don't know. I've been making these wreaths, you know, for your front door? I custom design them. I even made one for a man—he wanted troll dolls all over it."

Phoebe didn't want to demean her mother's handiwork. Olga did do some beautiful crafts. But that was hardly newsworthy. "I'm sure it was wonderful," Phoebe said. "How come you haven't made one for me?"

"Just wait your turn, young lady. You have a birthday coming up, and I've got some ideas."

Phoebe actually looked forward to receiving her mother's gift. The wreath would be one-of-a-kind and memorable, she was sure.

A terse knock on her door startled her. "Oh, Mama, there's someone at the door."

"The neighbor man? What's his name again?"

"Wyatt. I'm sure it's not him," Phoebe said as she headed for the door.

"I'll let you go, honey. We'll talk next week. I want you to tell me all about that TV show. And I want you to talk to the producer about my wreaths."

Phoebe stifled a groan as she ended the call. Once Olga got her teeth into something like this, she wouldn't let it go. Phoebe could just imagine Wyatt's reaction if she asked him to put her mother's wreaths on 'Heads Up'!

She pulled open the door, expecting to see Elise or Daisy or Frannie. They usually got together on the weekend for some type of exercise session. No one else she knew would pop in unannounced—

Except Wyatt, apparently. She looked down at her ratty bathrobe and bunny slippers, then at him in his sweatpants and T-shirt, his face unshaved, his hair still mussed from sleep—from her running her fingers through it. They could have been poster children for the Rumpled Saturday Morning disease.

Then she saw the plate he was holding, which was heaped with something that smelled awfully good.

Her stomach rumbled.

He thrust the plate at her. "I made French toast, and I had some left over."

Reflexively she took the plate, but she was too surprised to respond. Without another word, he turned and tromped back to his apartment.

For a few moments, Phoebe just stared. *What was that all about?*

She retreated into her kitchen and, never one to look a gift horse in the mouth, poured some syrup over the French toast and ate it. It was fantastic. Who'd have thought Wyatt could cook? Although, she did remember the Madisons saying something about their grandson being a whiz in the kitchen.

He'd seemed a little angry. Of course, when he'd seen her in her bathrobe he would have realized she didn't have an appointment. He'd caught her in her little white lie.

Was he insulted? Had she hurt his feelings by leaving in the middle of the night? She had a hard time picturing that. Still, she thought back to her checkered past. Once or twice a guy she'd thought she cared something for had slipped off into the night without a backward glance. And yes, it had hurt, briefly.

But those were guys she'd naively thought she might have some sort of future with. Surely Wyatt didn't have any such illusions about the two of them.

Still, now she felt bad. She'd been trying to protect them both from any further involvement, which might lead to more discomfort, heartache, disillusionment. And instead, she'd somehow angered or otherwise disappointed a man she very much wanted to remain on good terms with.

WYATT FELT like an idiot. He had no idea why he'd marched over to Phoebe's with that plate full of French toast. It had seemed important at the time that he make her understand she'd disappointed him by sneaking off in the night. A *man* who did something like that would be considered a tomcat of the worst order.

After he gave her the toast, though, he realized he'd been acting like a lovesick nut. Neither of them had made any promises. In fact, each had taken pains to make it clear to the other that they weren't looking for long-term anything, which pretty much relegated their lovemaking to one-night-stand status.

So why had it felt so different from other instances of casual, noncommittal sex in Wyatt's past?

By Sunday morning he'd almost put the episode into some kind of perspective. That was before he ran into Phoebe in the Mesa Blue weight room. He'd just finished a morning run, and he'd decided to visit the well-appointed weight room for some resistance training, which he'd been neglecting of late. He found Elise, Daisy and Phoebe working out to an aerobics videotape.

"Oh, hi, Wyatt!" Elise said cheerfully, while Phoebe studied an interesting spot on the ceiling. "Want to do flex-aerobics with us?"

"Ah, no thanks," he said, sitting down on the bench at one of the weight stations. He couldn't just leave; it would be too obvious that Phoebe got to him. So he sat there and endured seeing her in a neon-green leotard. It was a perfectly modest garment. But it revealed every one of her delicious curves, and when she jumped and stretched to the peppy music, she jiggled in all the right places.

Wyatt had to force himself to keep his eyes on the wall in front of him.

He moved to the bench press, where he could lie on his back and look up. He loaded enough weights onto the thing that he would really have to focus to lift it, then concentrated on his reps. Five…ten… His muscles burned, and sweat dripped off his face. Twelve…

Gradually he became aware that the music had stopped. So had the feminine chatter. Thank God. He'd outlasted them. He sat up and wiped the sweat off his face, then almost fell off the bench. Phoebe sat not five feet away, solemnly watching him.

"What are you doing here?" he blurted out, as if

she didn't have a perfect right to be in the weight room.

"Sorry, I didn't mean to startle you." She had her hair pulled back, and her skin glowed with a thin sheen of perspiration from her workout. Her cheeks were a healthy pink, her eyes bright and fiercely blue this morning, and every muscle looked firm and well-toned.

Unfortunately, he recalled exactly how that skin and those firm muscles had felt pressed against him.

He casually dropped his towel into his lap. "Are you waiting for the machine?"

"I was waiting for you to finish so we could talk."

He'd been afraid of that.

"Okay."

"Thanks for breakfast yesterday."

"No problem," he murmured. God, she would have to bring that up.

"I also wanted to apologize for leaving in the middle of the night," she said in a rush. "It wasn't very polite. I did it for you, though."

"For *me?*"

"I thought you'd prefer it that way. We both know that anything…long-term between us is completely unworkable."

"Agreed," he said quickly. This conversation made him feel distinctly like he was getting dumped, and he wanted to make sure it didn't end up that way.

"I thought leaving you a cheery note would save us from awkward goodbyes. We wouldn't have to mumble things about getting together again or calling or whatever."

Her explanation made perfect sense.

"I never meant to snub you or blow you off, though." She smiled slightly. "What we did might have been foolish, but I enjoyed our night together."

He wished she wouldn't look at him like that. He'd been about to master the hormones surging through his body—until she'd looked at him with remembered passion, her blue eyes dreamy, her tongue darting out unconsciously to moisten her lips. He would have to leave his towel in his lap the rest of his life.

"Me, too," he said simply. He guessed this wasn't the time to tell her how disappointed—no, *crushed*—he'd been to wake up alone yesterday.

"But when you brought over the French toast—"

"I made too much, and I didn't want it to go to waste, okay? Don't read anything into it."

"I won't," she said softly, sounding a bit hurt, making him regret his harshness. "I was just going to say I enjoyed it. I'm not a big breakfast eater normally, but I wolfed down every piece of that toast."

"Good."

"But it also made me realize I should have stayed and shared breakfast with you, like a proper, civilized overnight guest. Just because we aren't madly in love and planning to spend the rest of our lives together doesn't mean we can't enjoy each other's company once in a while."

Was she saying what he thought she was saying? For a few marvelous seconds, he thought she was suggesting they could make love on a regular basis. But she quickly disabused him of that notion.

"I didn't mean that the way it sounded," she blurted out rather desperately, her face turning even pinker. "Our...time together was great, and I won't forget it, but I don't think it's something we should repeat. I just meant that I don't want us to be uncomfortable with each other. I want us to be friends. I like you, we work together every day, I adore your grandparents, and for us to be anything less…or more… than friends is just completely unbearable. My life plans don't involve happily-ever-after, at least not in a domestic sense. And you aren't some starry-eyed kid with dreams of marrying the TV star.''

He gave her a pointed stare. ''You really are hung up on this age thing, aren't you.''

''I wasn't referring to your age! I was referring to emotional maturity.''

He realized he was nitpicking, trying to find fault with her argument when he knew damn well it was a perfectly good argument.

He sighed. ''Is there something I'm supposed to say here? You seem to have all the answers.''

''You don't have to say anything. Unless you disagree with me.''

Did he? Of course not. What she'd said made sense. They should be friends, no more, no less. But he couldn't quite get the words out to agree with her. He just wasn't very good at personal conversations. He was a guy, after all.

''Good,'' she said briskly. ''I'm glad we got this settled. I couldn't sleep last night, worrying if I'd offended you.''

''Consider me non-offended.''

''Then I think I'll soak in the hot tub for a while. Want to join me?'

''Ah, no,'' he said quickly. The last thing he

needed was to be confined to an intimate hot tub with
Phoebe in a swimsuit, her skin slick and wet.

"Okay, then. I'll see you tomorrow."

She got up and walked away without the slightest
notion that she was leaving behind a wreck of a man.
The woman tied him up in more knots than one of
his grandmother's macramé plant hangers.

What did he want from her? Just what the hell did
he want?

He did *not* want to be involved with her, physically
or emotionally. That much was certain. If anything
could deflect him from his crusade to make 'Heads
Up' the number-one-rated daytime talk show in the
country, Phoebe Lane could, and he absolutely
couldn't risk it. Too many people were depending on
his single-minded leadership.

Then, why couldn't he just look her in the eye and
say, *Phoebe, you are completely right. We had a good
time, but that's over and done with, and from now on
you are nothing to me but my employee and my temporary neighbor.*

Maybe it was because every time he looked her in
the eye, he couldn't help seeing the rest of her. And
the rest of her did crazy things to him. That wasn't
going to change, whether he took her to bed a hundred times, or pledged a hundred times to treat her as
just another co-worker.

PHOEBE FELT HER MUSCLES relaxing one by one as
she soaked in the hot, bubbly water in the hot tub.
The worst was over now. She'd rehearsed her speech
to Wyatt over and over so it would sound natural, and
thank God she was a good actress. Once or twice

she'd choked, forgotten her lines, but all in all she'd managed to assume a light tone. She'd done what she needed to do—put things right with Wyatt so they could continue working and living in close proximity without Friday night standing between them.

He'd wasted no time agreeing with her, she'd noticed. Though it might bruise her ego a bit, that was the result she'd been hoping for, right? Maybe now that they'd cleared the air, they could be more comfortable around each other. Maybe by making love one time, they'd dissipated the tension that had plagued them since day one.

And maybe California was going to drop into the ocean, making Mesa Blue beachfront property.

She heard the door to the wet area open. She tensed, thinking for one illogical moment that it might be Wyatt, that he'd changed his mind about joining her in the hot tub. She'd have *died* if he'd joined her. She would have had to sit on her hands.

Thankfully, it was Frannie who flapped into the wet area in her cat swimsuit. She smiled when she spotted Phoebe.

"Oh, I'm glad someone's in here," Frannie said, kicking off her thongs. "Every joint in my body is sore, and I know I need to soak, but I hate sitting in here alone."

"Me, too," Phoebe said, pleased to see anybody other than Wyatt. "Slide on in. Why are you so sore? You don't have arthritis, do you?"

"No, no, I'm just out of shape." Frannie eased herself into the steamy water, wincing at first, then smiling as she settled onto the seat and closed her eyes. "I went bowling with Bill last night. I haven't bowled in years, and I think I overdid it."

"Sounds like things are going okay for you and Bill."

Frannie grinned. "Great, as a matter of fact. That Jane Jasmine is so smart. Now, I'm a great bowler. I used to bowl three times a week. The old Frannie probably would have hidden that fact from Bill. I would have pretended not to know how to bowl so he could play the big strong man and show me how to do it, and then I would have let him win."

"But you didn't do that?"

"Heck, no. I told Bill I was going to give him a run for his money, pulled out my custom-made, monogrammed pink bowling ball, and beat the pants off him."

Phoebe gasped. "You're kidding!"

"Jane's book says to never hide or underplay your talents. So I didn't. And you know what?"

"What?" Inwardly, Phoebe cringed. Wasn't that exactly what she was doing with Wyatt, with practically the whole world? She was smart, she was on the dean's list, making almost straight A's in a tough field at a good university—and she was afraid to tell anybody.

"Bill loved it. He was so excited when I got two strikes in a row, he was crowing like a rooster. And when the last game was over and I'd won, he gave me a big hug and a kiss—and we went to dinner afterwards with some friends of his, and he bragged on me all through dinner."

"Well, of course. Men these days want to be with competent, capable, smart women." *Unless the woman is Phoebe Lane, in which case they don't care.*

"I know that's what *2001 Ways to Wed* says, but I didn't really believe it until I saw it for myself. From now on, I'm going to get out there and strut my stuff. No more false modesty. And you know what? I look *great* in a bathing suit."

Phoebe laughed. She was truly happy for Frannie and Bill, two of the nicest people she'd ever met. She only wished she could capture a fraction of Frannie's current self-confidence.

What would happen if she marched up to Wyatt and said, *I'll tell you why I spend so much time at the university, and it's not so I can chase premed students. I'm more than halfway to a degree in biochemistry, I'm planning to graduate* summa cum laude, *and then I'm going to get a loan and start my own all-natural cosmetics company.*

He would laugh. The whole thing still sounded ridiculous, even though she'd carried this dream around for years. She wished she didn't care what he thought, but she did.

Damn it, she did.

Chapter Nine

Elise laid out three photos of wedding dresses on the table. She sat with Phoebe and Daisy at The Prickly Pear for one of their semi-regular dinners, and she was in the throes of decision-making.

"I'm counting on you all to steer me right," Elise said. "Phoebe, you're the fashion expert here, and Daisy, you know all about color and texture. So which dress is right?"

Phoebe studied the three dresses. They were all beautiful. One was a fussy Victorian style with lots of flounces and ruffles, a real princess dress. One was a modern dress with a dramatic, off-the-shoulder cut, made out of a slick fabric without a hint of lace. The third was somewhere in between, traditional but not old-fashioned, satin trimmed in lace with a short train and a sort of retro-sixties empire waist.

Seeing the dresses put an odd ache into Phoebe's heart. Apart from her teenage fantasies of wanting to marry a movie star, Phoebe had never thought much about getting married. She'd always just assumed she wouldn't, because she'd never found a man she could relate to on anything but a physical level.

Except Wyatt, her devious brain reminded her.

True, she and Wyatt were friends of sorts. They'd gotten along fairly well this week, not quite as tense around one another, though their mutual awareness was never far from the surface. But they'd talked, and laughed, and Wyatt had even taken to asking Phoebe's opinion about ideas he had for the show. She supposed he considered her young and "plugged-in" enough that she could recognize cutting-edge when she saw it.

George came by to deliver their drink orders. He stopped to peer over Phoebe's shoulder at the dress pictures, then pointed at the modern one. "That's my favorite."

Phoebe rolled her eyes. "That's the model with the biggest breasts, George. She could be wearing a burlap sack and you'd pick her, as long as the sack had a plunging neckline."

"I still like that one best," George insisted, setting an iced tea in front of Phoebe and diet colas for the other two women.

As soon as he'd left, Elise plucked the picture of the modern dress off the table and wrinkled it up. "That takes care of that choice. What about the other two?"

"The Victorian is pretty," Daisy said, "but I'm afraid you'd just be lost in all those ruffles."

Phoebe nodded her agreement.

"What about the other?"

Phoebe studied the third dress. "I like it. But you have such a cute, slender waist, and this dress would hide it."

Glumly, Elise picked up the two photos and wrinkled them up, also. "This is all Jane Jasmine's fault. If I hadn't read her darn book, I never would have found James, and I wouldn't have to be planning a froufrou wedding."

Phoebe knew better than to believe Elise. She was having the time of her life, planning a big party where for once she got to be the center of attention, instead of one of a herd of sisters.

"My heart's breaking," Daisy said dryly.

"Oh, speaking of Jane Jasmine," Phoebe said, "guess who's going to be a guest next week on 'Heads Up.'" Phoebe took a sip of her drink and enjoyed the looks of surprise on her friends' faces.

"Jane Jasmine?" they said together.

"In the flesh. Apparently Wyatt's director read *2001 Ways to Wed* and was really impressed. She made Wyatt read it, and even he was impressed. He said she shows 'remarkable insight into the male psyche.'" Phoebe didn't add that Wyatt had also found the book on her bookshelf. She hadn't even revealed to her friends that Wyatt had been in her apartment, except to fix the burst hose. Normally the three women told each other everything, but Phoebe couldn't bear to share her and Wyatt's more intimate moments with anybody. It was still too painful.

"Yeah, well, Jane hasn't done much for me," Daisy groused. She'd been unusually glum ever since Elise's engagement party, Phoebe had noticed, and she was not as open to meeting new men as she'd been. Of course, given how some of her blind dates and fix-ups had turned out, Phoebe couldn't blame Daisy.

"Hey, I've got an idea," Phoebe said. "We're

bringing some other people onto the show with Jane—women who have actually found husbands using her book, and women who want to get married but haven't found Mr. Right. Daisy, I bet I could get you on—''

"No way!" Daisy exploded. "You want me to share with the whole country the fact that I can't catch a man?''

"It's a great idea!" Elise chimed in. "You'd probably get hundreds of men mailing in their marriage proposals. You could pick and choose among them.''

Daisy shuddered. "No, it's not even open for discussion.''

Phoebe and Elise looked at each other and shrugged.

WHEN THE THREE WOMEN returned from dinner, the doorman stopped Phoebe and took her aside. "There's someone here to see you. She wanted me to let her in your apartment, but of course I didn't, not without your say-so.''

"Thanks, Griffin.'' That was one of the things she loved about Mesa Blue—the security. As a TV actress, she'd had her share of weird letters and obsessive fans, though no one had bothered her in a while.

After waving goodbye to Daisy and Elise, she peered into the lobby's sitting area, at first not seeing anyone. Then a figure popped out from behind a column, and Phoebe almost fainted. "Mama!"

"Addy!" Olga Phelps rushed forward, enveloping a dazed Phoebe in a bear hug. After only a moment's hesitation, Phoebe returned the hug. She hadn't been home to visit since last summer, and she hadn't realized how much she missed her mother until this moment.

"Mama, what are you doing here? You look great!"

"I've lost a little weight, got a new haircut. My stylist says it makes me look ten years younger."

Phoebe sighed. Her mother was always looking for a magic youth potion. She did look great for her age, Phoebe had to admit. She was fifty, but no one would guess it.

"Come on," Phoebe said, hoisting one of Olga's bulging flowered suitcases. "Let's go up and get you settled in. How long can you stay? I'm afraid I won't be home very much..." She kept peppering her mother with questions as they headed for the elevator.

Olga informed her she would be staying through Tuesday, which meant five days. Phoebe could handle it, she decided. Her new job, with its shorter, more regular hours, had helped her to get control of her schedule. And she had no major tests or projects due for at least a week.

"Why didn't you let me know you were coming?" Phoebe scolded as they entered her apartment and switched on a light.

"It was a spur-of-the-moment decision." Olga looked around the apartment eagerly. "Oh, I like what you've done. But white furniture? Doesn't it get dirty?"

"I'm hardly home enough to get anything dirty."

"You just need one more thing to complete the decor." Olga put her suitcase on the sofa, opened it and pulled something out that was wrapped in news-paper.

When she unwrapped it, Phoebe smiled with pleasure. "A wreath."

And not just any wreath. It was made of movie film, artfully twisted and shaped so that it appeared to be a living thing. And all over the wreath were little symbols relevant to Phoebe's acting career—a tiny television; a copy of Phoebe's publicity photo shrunk down to less than an inch and put in a gold frame; Barbie-size ballet slippers; a minuscule Oscar statuette. There was even an itty-bitty movie slate with the words "Skin Deep" hand-painted in incredibly small letters.

"An early birthday present," Olga said.

Phoebe found a hammer and nails and proceeded to hang the wreath on her door right then and there. Her gaze strayed now and then toward Wyatt's door, hoping he wouldn't choose now to come home. The idea of Olga meeting Wyatt was kind of scary.

It took a few moments to figure out why. Wyatt was actually closer to Olga's age than he was to Phoebe's. And sometimes Olga went for younger men.

Holy cow, could she actually be jealous of her own mother?

"So, what made you decide to visit me so suddenly?" Phoebe asked a few minutes later as she and Olga shared coffee on the balcony.

"Well." Olga patted her hair and arched her eyebrows imperiously. "You, my dear, are not the only one who has show business connections. Since you wouldn't use your influence to get me on 'Heads Up,' I got my own self on."

Phoebe thought maybe she hadn't heard right.

"You're going to be on 'Heads Up'?" she repeated. "In the audience, you mean?"

"No, as a guest!"

Had Olga gone delusional? "Doing what?"

"Well, when I was watching the show the other day, they announced they were looking for a certain kind of person to be on the show."

Phoebe narrowed her eyes. "What kind of person?"

"They were looking for women who'd been trying to get married for more than five years, without success. For me, it's been more than twenty. So I qualified."

Phoebe felt the blood draining from her brain.

"I talked to a very nice man," Olga went on. "I can't remember his name—"

"Wyatt Madison?" Phoebe knew Wyatt personally talked to every guest before allowing them on the show.

"That's it. Wait, I thought that was your neighbor's name. The grandson?"

"It is," Phoebe said dully. "One and the same."

"Well, how about that. You didn't mention the connection before."

"It slipped my mind. Mama, are you telling me you're going to be on the show with Jane Jasmine?"

"Uh-huh, on Tuesday. Your Mr. Madison said she claimed she could help *anyone* find a husband, and I guess he thought I was the perfect test case. I faxed him a picture and a letter about what I wanted in a husband, and boom, I'm on the show. They even paid for my plane ticket."

She took a sip of her coffee, looking very smug.

Phoebe was going to kill Wyatt. He probably wasn't home from work yet—she hadn't seen his car in the lot. But when he did get home, she was going to let him know exactly how she felt about his manipulating her mother and giving Olga yet another dose of false hope.

WYATT WAS BUSHED. He'd spent all afternoon in delicate negotiations with an agent, trying to get him to allow his reclusive child-star client to come on the show. Apparently the child's mother was a fan of "Heads Up." She liked the way guests were treated on the show. But working out the details had been murder.

Just when he'd been about to head out the door, a technical problem had cropped up that had required Wyatt's special touch. Finally, he'd had to talk the high-strung Kelly through a personal crisis.

Now it was after midnight, late by even his standards. He couldn't wait to find his bed and crawl into it. He was confident that tonight, at least, he would be too tired to lie awake and remember what it had been like to have Phoebe in the bed beside him.

He came off the elevator and turned the corner— and skidded to a stop. Phoebe sat Indian-style in front of his door, arms crossed, looking like she could chew through plywood.

"Well, it's about time," she said, pushing herself to her feet.

"Is something wrong?"

"No, I was sitting in the hall waiting for you because I just can't get enough of you at work. *Of course something's wrong.*"

"You could have paged me."

"This conversation needs to take place in person."

Judging from the looks she gave him he might need a crash helmet for this conversation. What had he done wrong now?

He stuck his key in the door, and she followed him inside.

"Would you like to come in?"

"Don't be flip. We have a terrible problem."

He closed the door and turned on the light. "What is it, Phoebe?" he asked, all seriousness.

"How could you possibly have promised my mother you'd find her a husband? That was completely irresponsible of you."

"Huh?"

But she seemed not to hear him. Apparently she'd been seething with this dressing-down for some time, and she was going to have her say.

"You don't know my mother. She's practically planning the wedding already. Do you know how many times she's had her hopes dashed? Do you know how many men have used her, played her for a fool?"

He had no idea what Phoebe was talking about.

"It's only been in the past couple of years I've been able to convince her to stop throwing herself at every man she meets. She's finally gotten to the point where she's enjoying life, pursuing outside interests. She's actually very artistic. She's making these personalized wreaths. Anyway..."

Phoebe went on, but Wyatt had stopped at the word *wreaths*. Now, that rang a bell.

"Just one minute." He walked into the living

room, sat on the sofa and opened his briefcase on his lap. After shuffling a few papers while Phoebe looked on curiously, he found the one he wanted. "Are you talking about Olga Phelps? With the German-Jersey accent?"

"Who else? And it's a Danish-Jersey accent. She's from Denmark."

"I thought we were talking about your mother."

"We are!" Phoebe said impatiently. "You're not going to tell me you didn't know Olga was my mother, are you?"

"That's exactly what I'm telling you. She can't be, unless she gave birth to you when she was thirteen. And she couldn't have taught you how to talk."

Phoebe sighed. "She lied about her age. She's fifty. And I've had diction lessons, years of them."

"Really? You had a Jersey accent?"

"Wanna make sometin' of it, Chicago boy?"

Wyatt struggled not to laugh. She sounded like Sylvester Stallone. But he had to get back to the subject at hand. He studied Olga Phelps's picture. She was an undeniably attractive woman, with blond hair the exact color of Phoebe's, though it was short and feathered around her face, then teased into a beehive almost as high as Frannie's. And she wore a lot of makeup. He knew Phoebe wore makeup, too, but she applied it so skillfully he never noticed it.

"Convinced?" Phoebe asked, perching on the arm of the sofa, far too close for his peace of mind.

"If you say she's your mother, I'm sure she is, but I had no way of knowing."

"I can't believe she didn't mention it."

"Not a whisper."

"Well, I still don't approve of what you're doing. My mother doesn't need any pointers on husband-hunting. She's made a career out of it."

"An unsuccessful career, apparently. That's why Jane picked her to be on the show."

"Jane picked her?"

"I let Jane review all the people who sent in pictures and letters. She picked Olga first. She said if anyone needed her advice, it was your mother." Wyatt pulled a notebook from his briefcase and flipped to the page of notes he'd taken during his last phone call with Jane Jasmine. "She said Olga demonstrates classic self-esteem problems coupled with unreasonable expectations about romance and marriage."

Phoebe was silent. Wyatt suspected she saw the truth in Jane's assessment.

He returned his attention to the photo and statement Olga Phelps had sent in. Even he could see she tried too hard to be glamorous and sexy when she didn't have to. She was a natural beauty, like her daughter.

He glanced at the handwritten statement. "Hey, wait a minute. She says her only daughter's name is Adelaide."

"Uh, that would be me. Adelaide Phelps. I changed my name when I moved to L.A. when I was eighteen."

Wyatt let that bit of information sink in for a moment. Gorgeous, sophisticated Phoebe was really *Adelaide?*

Well, hell, what did that matter? The important thing was, she didn't sound so mad at him anymore. "Whatever. I had no intention of hurting or ridiculing your mother in any way. That's not what 'Heads Up' is about. Jane thinks she can help Olga overcome the self-destructive patterns she's been stuck in and, um—'' he read from his notes ''—'put her on a different, healthier path that will lead to her ultimate self-satisfaction.' Once she's happy with herself, she has a far greater chance of finding a compatible life partner.''

Phoebe sighed. ''I'd like to believe that.''

''Wait 'til you meet some of the women who followed Jane's advice and found husbands. They're like religious converts. The woman walks on water as far as they're concerned. Wouldn't you like for your mother to find similar success?''

''Of course I would. I just don't want to see her disappointed again. I happen to know of one woman who has followed all the advice in *2001 Ways to Wed,* and still has no husband to show for it.''

''Would she like to be on the show?'' Wyatt asked eagerly. He liked dissenting viewpoints.

''No, I asked her already. The point is, Jane doesn't work miracles on everybody.''

''Phoebe, let it go. Your mother chose to be on the show. She's really excited. Maybe it'll change her life for the better.''

Phoebe was silent for a moment. ''I guess you're right. I shouldn't be interfering in my mother's plans. I'm sure she wouldn't approve, any more than I do when she meddles in my life.''

''Then you'll stop chewing on me?'' Wyatt realized what he'd just said and suddenly wished Phoebe really would chew on him. Or nibble, rather. He had a whole closetful of reasons he and Phoebe shouldn't sleep together anymore, but right now he couldn't recall a single one, not when she was this close.

Decisively, he put everything back in his briefcase and closed it. If she didn't take that as a signal and move away from him, he wasn't going to be responsible for his actions.

He set the briefcase on the floor. Phoebe didn't budge.

"Was there anything else?" he asked almost crossly.

"I think I owe you an apology. I guess I overreacted."

"You were concerned about your mother. Nothing wrong with that."

"But I should have known you wouldn't do anything exploitive on the show. You're not like every other TV guy I've known. You have scruples, and you treat everyone with dignity. I've seen enough now to know how you operate."

"You think I'm a smooth operator?" He looked up at her, seeing a warmth and openness that surprised him. All week they'd been friendly, but she'd maintained a certain reserve that had kept him at arm's length. That reserve didn't seem to be anywhere in evidence.

She smiled. "I think you're flirting with me."

"It's pretty damn hard not to." His thinking about Phoebe had changed a lot over the past couple of weeks. How could he ever have suspected Phoebe saw him as a stepping-stone to stardom? He supposed he'd had so many negative experiences with grasping, teasing, insincere women, it had taken him a long time to recognize a real diamond when it fell in his lap.

And speaking of things falling into his lap... He put his arm around Phoebe's slender hips and gave the slightest of tugs, sending her sprawling right across his thighs.

"Wyatt!" she cried through her giggles.

He settled her against him more comfortably, and she didn't struggle. "Don't tell me you didn't know what you were doing, sitting on the arm of the sofa like that."

"Oh, sure, blame the victim."

"I'm the victim here. Tempted beyond the bounds of human decency by a witch, a siren."

She ruffled his hair, then stroked his face. "Are you calling me a witch?"

"A Lorelei." He wondered if she would get the reference. If she went to L.A. to be an actress when she was eighteen, she must not have gone to college. Of course, she was taking classes now, but he assumed she was only dabbling.

"I keep telling you, I'm Danish, not German—and I've never been near the Rhine."

"You've been reading German folklore?" he asked, genuinely surprised.

"My mother read folktales to me when I was a child."

"Ah." He could picture the child Phoebe—or Adelaide, as she was then—curled up in bed, her pretty mother reading from a book of folklore. Only, in his mind the mother became Phoebe and the child was her daughter. His daughter.

The mental picture gave him a peculiar ache. He

didn't even understand why he'd thought of something so preposterous, much less why it bothered him. He'd never longed for marriage or family, and he wasn't going to start now.

"Wyatt? You have an odd look on your face."

He didn't doubt it. That was the strangest break from reality he'd ever had. He supposed a gorgeous woman in his lap could have peculiar effects. "If I look strange, it's because I'm dying to kiss you. But we do sort of have this understanding."

"Yeah, we do," she said glumly.

"Wasn't that understanding your idea?"

"You agreed to it."

"I agreed not to touch you? Temporary insanity. Anyway, you're the one who started this by not maintaining a proper distance from me. If you're close enough I can smell your perfume and see individual eyelashes, that's too close."

"I'll move." She started to wiggle out of his lap, which only inflamed him further. He was stiff as a poker, and there was no way she wouldn't know that.

"You just stay where you are," he said, holding on tighter.

"Only if you absolve me."

"You're absolved. It's all my fault. Everything."

"If only more men knew how to speak those words…" She didn't finish the thought. She was too busy kissing him.

Her mouth was a thing of wonder. He explored it at a more leisurely pace than he had before, invading with his tongue, then retreating to nip at her full, soft lips, kissing hard, kissing soft.

Before long they were lying on the couch instead

of sitting. He was on his back, and she was on top of him. When she wasn't kissing him, she was tickling his ear, playing with his hair, running her tongue along his neck.

"Um, Phoebe, wait." He couldn't believe he was doing this. He would have to resign his macho-guy membership.

Phoebe crossed her arms over his chest and propped her chin on them. "What?" she asked with exaggerated innocence. With her hair all mussed and her eyes heavy-lidded with passion, she was just about the most beautiful thing he'd ever seen.

"Nothing has really changed…has it?"

She lowered her eyes. "No."

"I'm still not good boyfriend material. I'm a slave to that TV show. Furthermore, I'm very set in my ways. Been alone too long. I wouldn't know how to make room for a regular woman in my life."

"I know," she said impatiently, sitting up.

"I'd disappoint you."

"I have no expectations, all right? I just…want you. Is it so hard to understand that I might want to make love to you without expecting anything in return?"

Frankly, it was almost impossible. He'd never met a woman yet who didn't have an agenda. With Phoebe it might not be acknowledged, but he firmly believed women simply weren't hard-wired to enjoy casual sex the same way men did.

Ah, hell, who was he kidding? "It's me I'm worried about," he finally said. "I'm the one with the old-fashioned expectations. I feel like I'm being unfair to you."

"Why don't you let me worry about me?"

"Because that's the man's job."

"You are old-fashioned."

He wouldn't argue. "Maybe I'm worried about my own expectations, too. If any woman could make me change my priorities, you could. But you've made it pretty clear you don't want to be tied down yet. You could hurt me pretty bad."

"Now you're teasing. I can't imagine my dashing your fantasy of a white picket fence."

Then she didn't know him very well. What would she think, he wondered, if she were privy to that bedtime-story fantasy he'd entertained a few minutes ago? Sure, he thought about white picket fences, in unguarded moments.

"So," he said, "is there an argument I could use that would make you get up and go home?"

"You could say, 'Phoebe, I am not interested in making love. Go home and stop throwing yourself at me, you're making a fool of yourself.'"

"You want me to tell a bald-faced lie?"

"I don't want you to lie. But those are the magic words, whether they're true or not, that would get rid of me." She played with his lower lip, touching it gently with the pad of her finger. He took it into his mouth and sucked it.

It would take a pair of pliers and three strong men to pull those words out of his mouth. He wasn't going to send her away. They were going to make love, though nothing was settled. They would have all the same regrets, all the same problems they had before.

When Phoebe kissed him again, he flat out didn't care.

Chapter Ten

Phoebe didn't care about anything at the moment except being with Wyatt. They'd made love once before and had still managed to work together. No reason they couldn't do it again. She just couldn't keep away from him.

When he'd so patiently explained what his hopes were for Olga, how he wanted to help her and the other lovelorn guests that would be coming on the show, her anger had evaporated like summer rain in Phoenix.

He'd been completely sincere, and she should know. In L.A. she'd been inundated with every smarmy line, every sob story, every act of false humility, all to get her into bed. She could smell a line from a mile away. She knew when someone was trying to manipulate her. Wyatt might play the part of the tough producer, but he had a heart as big as a bowling ball. He would be thrilled if Jane could help Olga and the other husband-less ladies find happiness—and not just because it would boost ratings.

"Just tonight, Wyatt. Just one more time." She knew she sounded desperate.

"Whenever, however you want it," he said, sounding equally desperate. In a deft maneuver he flipped her onto her back and was looming over her. "You didn't honestly think I would say no, did you?"

He kissed her, hard, and her nipples tightened beneath her clothes. She'd worn short overalls and a tube top tonight, not out of any desire to turn Wyatt on but because that happened to be what was handy. Now she was glad of her choice, because Wyatt could slide his hands inside the overalls, give the tube top one healthy yank, and her breasts were completely exposed to him.

He pushed himself up to admire his handiwork. "Now, this is how a woman ought to wear overalls."

"You're a horrible sexist."

"Just an honest man."

Though he was teasing, she knew it was true. He'd never been anything but honest with her. She wished she could say the same for herself.

She wanted to confide in him about her goals and dreams. He was a savvy businessman; he would probably have all kinds of helpful advice about how to start her business. But not even her best friends knew the extent of her ambitions, and hiding them had become second nature.

Given the uncertain nature of her relationship with Wyatt, she didn't dare open herself up to that extent. She trusted him completely with her body. She trusted him to take care of her on the job. But she couldn't quite trust him with her soul.

He gave her nipple a gentle squeeze, and she forgot all about goals and dreams and cosmetics. It was pretty hard to do anything except live in the moment when she was in Wyatt's arms.

He unfastened the shoulder straps of her overalls and pushed them out of the way, then kissed her breasts with a thoroughness that had been lacking during their previous encounter. They'd been much too rushed to take their time.

But, oh, what they'd been missing. Phoebe squirmed as he lavished attention on first one breast, then the other, rolling his mouth over the nipples until they pebbled into hard peaks. Her whole body was on fire, with a particularly noticeable warmth between her thighs. But Wyatt seemed in perfect control, and she had a strong feeling he was going to enjoy driving her crazy with wanting before he brought her to satisfaction.

While he was sucking on her breasts, he managed to undo the side buttons of her overalls. Before she knew it, he'd slid the denim garment effortlessly down her legs. How had he managed that? she wondered. Even she couldn't take them off that easily when she was alone in her bedroom at home. With a surge of jealousy, she realized he'd probably undressed lots of women.

She made a token effort to unbutton the gray cotton shirt he wore, which still looked crisp and smelled like starch despite the long day he'd put in. But she was easily distracted when he moved down to kiss her stomach, so she gave up trying to undress him. He'd work it out on his own. She was drowning in sensations, almost paralyzed, and he would have to orchestrate things from here.

Her brain wasn't completely paralyzed, she discovered. "What are we going to do about protection?" They'd used his one and only condom a week ago.

He chuckled. "Not to worry." He moved away from her. She raised herself to see what he was doing, and found him rummaging in his briefcase.

"You keep...*those* in your briefcase?"

He sat down on the edge of the sofa by her feet and calmly took off his shoes and socks. "I found some more in my closet. And I threw one in my briefcase because I had this fantasy about you and me in conference at the studio—behind a locked door."

"Wyatt. I thought we'd agreed."

"It was a fantasy, okay? But I figured it wouldn't hurt to be prepared in case the impossible happened."

Now that Phoebe thought about it, it didn't sound so impossible. In fact, it sounded downright delicious. "We could do it on your desk," she said in a naughty whisper.

He stood up and unzipped his pants, casually dropping them and kicking them aside. He wore navy blue briefs. She'd been too dazed before to pay attention. Now she did. How could she not, when the evidence of her effect on him was so clearly, wonderfully obvious?

"We could do it on the set with a spotlight on us," he said as casually as if they were discussing a trip to the supermarket. "After everyone's gone home for the day."

A thrill ran up Phoebe's spine. "We could do it in Kelly's dressing room, on that ridiculous fur rug she has."

Wyatt froze in the act of unbuttoning his shirt.

"Phoebe, stop. I won't be able to keep a straight face anywhere in the studio if we keep this up."

She laughed. "We could drag Kelly's fur rug into the studio, turn on a red spotlight, maybe borrow a bottle of wine from that locked cabinet in the commissary—"

He shrugged out of his shirt and was on her in a flash. "No more."

Then he was kissing her, and she felt no more urges to laugh or giggle. Wyatt was very serious about his lovemaking. Very thorough. Very single-minded. Like he was about his work.

She wouldn't mind if he put his work first, she thought desperately. She wouldn't mind if he worked until midnight every night. She wouldn't mind if he could only spare her a half-hour every other Sunday. If only, when he was with her, he would focus on her like this, to the exclusion of everything else.

It was the most erotic turn-on she'd ever experienced.

Slightly frantic now, they both removed the last obstacle of clothing between them. Phoebe took a moment to appreciate what a splendid male animal Wyatt was before she opened herself to him, but he didn't accept her silent invitation right away. First he made sure she was thoroughly kissed in the most intimate way possible. He made sure she was as worked up as a woman could get.

He made her beg.

Finally, when she thought she would scream, he entered her in one quick, possessive thrust that branded her as his.

Compared to his previous gentleness, he was almost rough, taking his pleasure, and she reveled in it. He might have been trying to make her lose control, but he was the one behaving like a savage now.

And she loved it. She loved this side of him, the slightly wild sexual conqueror.

With that thought she went over the edge with a cry of pure, unbridled ecstasy, which was followed almost immediately by Wyatt's final, exultant thrust.

For long moments afterward they lay together, panting, damp with perspiration though the room was well cooled. After a couple of minutes they pulled apart and found a semi-comfortable position, with Phoebe lying against Wyatt's chest.

Finally Phoebe spoke. "Oh, my God."

"What?" He sounded concerned.

"We did it on your grandparents' sofa."

"Oh, my God."

Another long silence. Then she said, "Wyatt?"

"Mmm."

"I can't stay with you tonight."

That got his attention. He pushed himself up on one elbow and peered into her eyes. "I'm not letting you leave. I'll tie you to the bedposts."

"Hmm. Interesting though that sounds, my mother is staying with me. She'll wonder where I am, and I can't tell her I slept with you."

"Why not? She seemed a fairly modern, liberated lady to me."

"You're not her daughter. She's as protective of her only-born as a she-bear, and unless you're prepared to explain why you're not marching me down the aisle posthaste, you'd better let me leave."

"Ah."

She could see he most certainly did not want to make any explanations to Olga.

"You're expecting to keep our relationship a secret, then?"

Wyatt's use of the word *relationship* startled her. For a moment she froze and just stared at him, dumbfounded.

"Or are you going to look me in the eye and tell me we made yet another mistake, and this isn't going to happen ever again?"

She honestly hadn't thought that far ahead.

"Make no mistake, Phoebe, this is going to happen again. And again and again, if I have anything to say about it. Denying the attraction, avoiding each other, feeling uncomfortable around each other, takes more energy than just giving in, don't you think?"

He had a point, but she still wasn't sure how to respond. *Relationship?* That sounded kind of scary. Delicious, but scary.

He brushed her cheek with his finger and softened his tone. "You scare the hell out of me, you know that?" he said, echoing her thoughts. "I can't believe some of the things that come out of my mouth when I'm around you."

"Believe me, I understand."

"I'm not good at dealing with gray areas. I like to nail things down, define exactly where we stand."

"So you don't have to think about it."

"Well, maybe," he agreed. "But it would make things easier if we both knew what to expect. Then we could just…proceed."

And Phoebe was just the opposite. She wanted to stick her toe in the water and test the temperature, do things on a trial basis—so she could retreat if she had to, preferably without losing face or breaking any promises.

"Can't we just play it by ear?" she ventured.

"Something tells me you're a little commitment-shy. Even tiny commitments, like a regular Saturday night date."

"Is that what you want?" she asked quickly. His proposal didn't sound so bad. In fact, she kind of liked it.

"Would you agree to it?"

"Maybe," she said coyly.

He twisted a strand of her hair around his finger. "I'm not sure once a week is enough. You're highly addictive."

"How about Tuesdays and Saturdays?" she countered. She couldn't believe she was negotiating a dating schedule. But if that's what it took to make Wyatt comfortable, she'd do it. She enjoyed a little more spontaneity in her love life, when she had one, but maybe she and Wyatt could work up to that.

"I think I could manage that."

"Great. You like music?"

"Sure."

"I know this great little club where they have the best bands. We could go there Saturday."

"It's a deal." He kissed her on the nose to seal the bargain. Then he let her get up and get dressed, but only reluctantly.

"I'll warn you, I'm not good at sneaking around," he said. "If you insist on keeping our relationship a secret I'll try, but—"

"Not a secret," she said. "But I don't want to

advertise it, especially at work. You are my boss, after all, and that can get a little sticky. I know from experience.''

"Fair enough.''

"And I'll let my mother know. In my own way.''

"Okay. What about your friends?''

"Elise and Daisy will figure it out. They've got a sixth sense where these things are concerned.'' They would want details, too, which she did not intend to provide. After having her romantic liaisons detailed in one of the lesser tabloids, she turned into a very private person when it came to her personal life.

PHOEBE WASN'T too far off in her estimation of Elise's and Daisy's sixth sense. She didn't say one word, but when the three of them, plus her mother, met at The Prickly Pear Friday night, as was their habit, it didn't take them five minutes to pick up on her change of mood.

"You're humming,'' Elise said, after they'd given their order to George. "What's got you so perky?''

"Oh, nothing much,'' Phoebe said. Of course, her face immediately heated up when she fibbed.

"Nothing much?'' Daisy repeated. "You're blushing.''

"I bet *I* know,'' Olga said in a singsong voice.

"Mama…'' Phoebe implored.

"It's Wyatt!'' Daisy and Elise said together.

Phoebe nearly choked on her iced tea. "How did you come to that conclusion?''

"I saw him this morning,'' Daisy said. "I had to get to the gallery early, and he was on his way to his car. He smiled and waved, and he had a spring to his step I've never noticed before.''

"And I saw him as he got home from work," Elise said. "I passed him on the stairs. When I asked him how he was doing, he said, 'Fantastic.' Only one thing I can think of changes a man overnight from a grouchy, hibernating bear to Mr. Congeniality.''

"He got the weekly ratings yesterday," Phoebe said. "'Heads Up' is first in its time slot.'' Which was true. But Elise and Daisy weren't buying it.

"Oh, just tell them," Olga said. "You can't keep a man like Wyatt secret for long, and I don't know why you'd want to.''

Phoebe sighed. "Yes, Wyatt and I have been spending time together—but it's nothing serious," she added quickly. "We're just having fun. Wyatt's new in town, he doesn't know anyone, and the Madisons did expect me to help him get settled into Phoenix.''

"That's great, Phoebes," Elise said, squeezing Phoebe's arm. "I thought from the beginning there might be a little spark there.''

"I told you so," Daisy added. "I knew he was smitten.''

"Now don't you guys go making wedding plans. This is not some fairy tale, I'm no princess, and Wyatt certainly isn't Prince Charming. I doubt this thing will last through the summer. What with working together, we'll probably get tired of each other.''

"My, what a bright, sunshiny outlook you have," Elise said dryly. "Nothing like low expectations.''

"I'm just being realistic," Phoebe argued. "My expectations aren't low, they're reasonable. And if things don't…*when* things don't work out, I won't have so far to fall.'' She'd learned the hard way about falling, with Joel. She'd lost that starry-eyed attitude a long time ago, and she had no intention of bringing it back.

''I just have one question,'' Daisy said. ''If you and Wyatt are an item, how come you're not with him tonight?''

''How come Elise isn't with James?'' Phoebe countered.

''We're meeting later,'' Elise said.

''Well, that's fine for you. You're getting married. But I have no desire to attach myself to Wyatt at the hip. We both have our own lives to live.''

Then why did she suddenly, desperately, wish she could be with him? She'd seen him just this morning, but at work she couldn't touch him, kiss him, laugh with him. She'd thought that giving in to their desires would decrease the tension and make her stop thinking about him so much. In fact, the opposite was true.

She was rapidly becoming obsessed with the man.

WYATT DID HIS BEST to honor Phoebe's wishes about privacy. At work he resisted the urge to touch her, even innocently, though it just about killed him to do so. Even so, by the end of the first day the whole crew knew something was up with him and Phoebe, especially when they both got a case of the giggles talking to Kelly in her dressing room, assiduously avoiding even a peek at the fur rug.

Phoebe seemed okay with it when Phyllis, the director, made a teasing remark, so he tried not to worry.

He didn't need more worries in his life. Running this show and trying to juggle dozens of people's expectations and ego trips was aging him. At least the ratings were good so far—steadily increasing. He must be doing something right.

On Friday night, for the first time since moving to Phoenix, he found himself bored. No budgets or forecasts to do, no phone calls to make. He gave the condo a good cleaning, in anticipation of bringing Phoebe here tomorrow night, but that only took an hour. He made himself a hamburger for dinner, gave all his grandmother's plants some plant food, and dutifully talked to the cacti. That took him to eight o'clock.

He worked out in the Mesa Blue weight room, hoping he might run into Phoebe or one of her friends there, but the room was deserted. He showered.

Nine o'clock.

Maybe two nights a week weren't enough.

He decided to call Phoebe. He could at least finalize their plans for tomorrow. But her answering machine picked up.

Where was she? he fumed. Out with one of her college beaux?

He knew his anger was unreasonable. He had no claim to Phoebe, just as she had none on him. He could pick up the phone right now and call that cute brunette who worked at the deli where he often had lunch. She'd thoughtfully included her phone number with his hoagie sandwich earlier this week.

But the brunette held little appeal. It was blond hair he thought of now—long, straight, white-gold silk he could swim in.

He went to bed with a boring book, hoping it would dull him to sleep.

PHOEBE DRESSED with more than usual care for her Saturday date with Wyatt. She wanted to look her best—she wanted to look hot. But she didn't want to look like a teenager. So she tried on one outfit after another, while her mother gave her a running commentary.

"What about this?" Phoebe asked as she stood in front of the mirror in red hip-hugger jeans, platform clogs and a ribbed halter top.

"Beautiful," Olga said. "If you want to look like a teen hooker. All you need is a ring in your navel."

She didn't tell her mother she'd actually had her navel pierced when she lived in L.A. She'd done it for Joel. After they broke up, she decided it didn't suit her and quit wearing the ring. She still had a tiny scar.

Next she tried on a pair of baggy pants and an oversize T-shirt.

"Lovely," Olga said. "Except no one can tell you're a girl. Don't you have something in between? Gawd, not those overalls," she said quickly, when Phoebe reached for a lilac pair. Phoebe hid a secret smile, remembering how she'd wanted to peel off her overalls during her first confrontation with Wyatt.

She finally settled on snug black pants, a crop top that showed only a narrow strip of skin at her waist, and flat-heeled boots. She wouldn't set the fashion world on fire, but she wouldn't scare Wyatt.

He knocked on her door promptly at ten. He'd sounded a little dubious when she'd suggested that time, but when she'd explained that The Pit, the club she wanted to take him to, didn't really get going until midnight, he'd agreed. She liked that about him: his flexibility. Joel had always wanted to be right.

She opened the door, taking a moment to appreciate the visual impact. He wore a pair of starched khakis, a forest-green shirt, polished loafers—and a tie. A grown-up preppie. Apparently he'd taken more than a little care with his wardrobe, because even at work he didn't wear a tie.

He spent no small amount of time studying her before finally smiling in approval. "Hi."

"Hi, yourself. Come in and meet my mother."

"Gee, I haven't been through this ritual since high school."

She touched his forearm in a small gesture of reassurance. Olga would approve.

Olga stepped out of the kitchen, wiping her hands on a dishcloth, as Phoebe led Wyatt into the living room.

"Oh, hello," she said, as if her appearance hadn't been calculated down to the last second. "You must be Wyatt."

"Hello, Ms. Phelps." Wyatt extended his hand to her, and she shook it a bit awkwardly. "I'm looking forward to having you on the show."

"I'm looking forward to being there," she cooed, batting her eyelashes. "My, Phoebe said you were handsome, but she didn't tell the half of it."

Phoebe rolled her eyes. When Olga turned on the full force of her feminine charm, it was a thing to be feared. But Wyatt just rolled right along with it.

"And Phoebe didn't tell me how pretty you are. Your photo doesn't do you justice."

Olga patted her blond, puffy hair and batted her false eyelashes. "Oh, how you do go on."

Phoebe decided she'd better get Wyatt out of there before they were hip-deep in treacle. "We'd better get going."

"You won't keep her out too late, will you, Wyatt?" Olga admonished.

"Mama, I haven't had a curfew since I was seventeen. Do *not* wait up for me."

"Of course not, dear," Olga said complacently, but Phoebe knew her mother would sleep with one ear open.

As soon as she was alone with Wyatt, she let out a pent-up breath. "She makes me crazy."

"She seems perfectly charming and delightful to me."

"You're not her daughter. Wyatt..." she began, as they stepped onto the elevator. "You look great."

"You look hot. I hope I don't have to fight off other guys."

Phoebe hoped not, too. Usually when she went to a club—and she didn't do it very often anymore—she spent a good deal of time fending off unwanted male attention. There was something about yards of blond hair that raised testosterone levels. Yet she was too vain to cut it off. Though she'd turned her back on Hollywood and claimed disdain for a world that valued looks and sex appeal above everything, she nevertheless made the most of her own physical assets.

Something to ponder.

She settled into the butter-soft leather interior of Wyatt's Jaguar and gave him directions to The Pit, as he effortlessly guided the powerful machine through light traffic.

The streets grew more congested as they approached downtown. Tucked away in the back streets lived a party district that came alive only after dark. Funky restaurants, off-beat clubs and tattoo parlors lined the narrow streets.

"I never even knew this neighborhood was here," Wyatt said as he pulled his car into a vacant lot that had been transformed into parking. A guy with about six rings in his ear collected five dollars from Wyatt, promising security.

Wyatt looked dubious, but he paid the guy, pulled into his assigned spot and cut the engine.

Phoebe laid a hand on his arm. "Before we go, could you do one thing?"

"What?"

"Lose the tie."

Chapter Eleven

Wyatt paused a beat, then chuckled as he complied with Phoebe's request. "I guess this isn't quite the symphony, is it."

"Do you go to the symphony?"

"Not since I've been in Phoenix, but I used to go hear the Chicago Pops all the time. I even had season tickets. Do you like classical music?"

"I'm not sure," Phoebe said uneasily. "I've never really listened to it."

"We can fix that. If you're any kind of music lover, you have to at least appreciate the masters, even if you don't become a huge fan. Mozart, Bach, Beethoven—they're at the root of every piece of music we've listened to since their time."

"Uh-huh," Phoebe said, and Wyatt couldn't tell if she didn't believe him or was simply bored by the topic. He realized maybe he was sounding like a pompous jerk. Women didn't go out on dates to be lectured to.

They got out of the car. Phoebe didn't wait for him to open her door, thank God. He liked her self-sufficiency, her independence. It was those qualities that were going to make this relationship work. A clinging vine would want his undivided attention seven days a week, and he simply didn't have that to give.

Although, he thought, *the way Phoebe looks tonight, I wouldn't mind seeing her twenty-four-seven.* He'd gone out with attractive women before—some of them even beautiful. But he'd never succumbed to that purely male indulgence of believing his own worth was being measured by the physical appeal of the woman on his arm.

Until tonight.

As they approached the club, foot traffic got heavier, and Phoebe took his arm so they could stay together. Virtually every male who passed gave her an appreciative once-over, and then they looked at Wyatt, sizing up his worthiness. A few even gave him a nod, silently approving his male prowess in capturing such a prize.

His caveman instincts came to the surface. He was pretty hot stuff.

A large crowd had formed in front of The Pit, an unremarkable brick-front building with blacked-out windows and lots of purple neon. A big-bellied bouncer type in baggy, striped pants, a leather vest and no shirt was apparently controlling entry into the club.

"Uh-oh," Wyatt said. "Maybe we should have gotten here earlier."

"Not to worry," Phoebe said with a confident smile. She sailed right through the crowd, which seemed to part for her as if she were royalty. Wyatt followed in her wake.

The frowning bouncer suddenly found a big grin when he spotted Phoebe.

"Phoebe, darling, where have you been?" He leaned down and air-kissed her cheek. "Go right in." He moved aside to give her access to the door.

Phoebe gave Wyatt an I-told-you-so look over her shoulder, then reached for the door. But the bouncer stepped in front of Wyatt. "Not you, pops."

Phoebe screeched to a halt and gave the bouncer a scathing look. "He's with me."

"Oh, sorry," the bouncer said, almost bowing and scraping. He quickly moved aside to let Wyatt into the club.

"Pops?" Wyatt said, once they were inside the door. *"Pops?"*

"Oh, forget him," Phoebe said, taking Wyatt's hand. "Let's see if we can find a table."

Wyatt was still seething. At thirty-nine he was no longer a kid, but he wasn't ready for a wheelchair and Geritol, either. In fact, he still thought of himself as kind of studly.

As they wove their way through the packed club, Wyatt's feelings of studliness decreased by the moment. He was the oldest guy here. He searched the crowd for a hint of gray hair, a wrinkle or two, but clearly this was where Phoenix's beautiful people gathered. Make that *young* and beautiful.

Here he was, producer of a show about everything cutting edge, yet in this place he felt decidedly clueless. *Old* and clueless.

With unerring instinct, Phoebe led them to the only available table, which overlooked a sunken dance floor. On a small stage, a band was setting up.

The moment they sat down, a cocktail waitress appeared in very short shorts, a sports bra and something that looked like a chain-mail vest.

"What can I get you to drink?" She teetered slightly on her four-inch platform shoes.

"Club soda with lemon, please," Phoebe said.

"Orange juice," Wyatt said. The waitress looked at him blankly. He amended his order. "A screwdriver, hold the vodka."

"Oh, okay." She disappeared.

Phoebe smiled. "Not a health nut, I guess."

That was the last easy conversation they had for some time, because the band started up. Or at least, Wyatt assumed the noise emanating from the amplifiers was supposed to be music. It sounded to him more like a dozen cats thrown into a room full of pit bulls, and the decibel level had to be damaging his hearing.

But the crowd seemed to like it. The dance floor filled immediately and soon became one writhing, pulsating glob of youthful gyrations. Wyatt couldn't even tell who was partnered with whom. The dancers weren't holding on to each other, but they rubbed up against each other in blatant sexual abandon.

Phoebe smiled and tapped her foot to the music.

He tried to find the humor. He'd spent his early youth in crowded, smoky clubs, getting his ears blasted out by garage bands trying to reproduce the sounds of Arrowsmith, Springsteen and ZZ Top.

He'd never dressed as weirdly as these kids, though. His generation, sandwiched between the fashion nightmare of the '70s and the retro '90s, had done their rebelling in khakis, button-downs and Topsiders.

Phoebe tried to yell something to him, but he couldn't understand her. Finally he realized she was pointing at the dance floor. She leaned across the table, giving him an entrancing glimpse of cleavage, and spoke loudly into his ear. "Look who's here!"

He looked, and there were Kelly and Kurt, right in the thick of the dancers.

He was relieved to know members of his team were frequenting this den of the oh-so-hot-and-trendy—so he wouldn't have to. If the sound decibels didn't get to him, the cigarette smoke would.

The waitress brought their drinks, and wrote down his total on a pad of paper and showed it to him. He paid her, including a generous tip, figuring she deserved it just for surviving this place night after night.

The band paused, and Phoebe clapped and whistled. Wyatt dutifully clapped.

"Do you want to dance?" Phoebe asked.

"Um, no, not really," he replied. Though he wouldn't mind rubbing his body against Phoebe's, he didn't know the moves, and he refused to go out on the dance floor and look like a turkey. "But you can if you'd like. I'm not the jealous type."

He could tell she wanted to. "Maybe I'll dance with Kelly and Kurt," she said.

Group dancing?

"Don't you like to dance?"

"Sure, I just—I'd rather watch for now."

The band screeched to life again. Phoebe gave his hand a "be right back" squeeze, then worked her way onto the dance floor.

He enjoyed watching her dance. She knew how to move her body, that was for sure. She laughed with Kurt and Kelly, as they all flowed with the beat. And when that song was over and a slower one started, all three headed back to the table. Kurt and Kelly dragged up chairs and ordered drinks.

"I never thought I'd see you here," Kurt said to Wyatt. "Doesn't seem like your kind of gig."

"I'm pretty adaptable," Wyatt said, which was true. He could be a chameleon when he wanted to be. But this place was so far removed from his normal sphere of reality, he didn't know how to adapt.

They couldn't talk much while the music was blaring, but when the band took a break Wyatt leaned back and observed his three younger friends talking about music.

He didn't recognize a single song they mentioned, or the names of the artists—except he'd heard of Koi Paloi because they'd been on "Heads Up" his first week in Phoenix.

When the band started again, Kelly and Kurt jumped up and headed for the dance floor. Phoebe gave him a sweet smile, stood, and offered her hand.

Okay, so he'd dance with her.

But instead of heading for the dance floor, she made for the exit.

The cool night air felt like heaven. "Why're we leaving?" he asked.

"Because you were miserable."

"'Miserable' is a bit strong. 'Out of my element' is more like it."

"So you're not really into alternative music?" she

asked, swinging hands with him as they ambled down the sidewalk toward the parking lot.

"If that's what that band was playing, no."

"What music do you listen to, then? Other than classical."

He suspected that if he admitted he listened to classic rock, she would be appalled. "Why don't I just show you?"

She smiled. "Okay."

Wyatt knew of a little jazz bar that was just on the fringe of downtown, not too far. Phyllis had taken him there for a drink after one of their late-night planning sessions, and he'd loved the soft, smoky music and the low-key atmosphere. Plus, the music wasn't so loud that you couldn't talk over it.

He found a parking place right in front. Phoebe looked around as they entered, her eyes bright and curious.

They had no trouble finding a table. The fifty-something waitress wore a long black dress and spike heels. Phoebe ordered coffee, and Wyatt switched to club soda. Then he settled back to let the music warm his blood. Saxophone music was just downright sexy.

Now he felt in his element. He studied the other patrons. Plenty of silver hair here. And neckties. In fact, he was probably one of the youngest people in the bar. And Phoebe was definitely the youngest.

She gazed at the stage, but there were no flashing lights or gyrating singers to hold her visual attention. Just four guys in dark glasses focusing on their instruments. Three couples danced cheek-to-cheek on the postage-stamp dance floor.

Phoebe's eyelids drooped, and her chin almost fell off her hand where she rested it.

Wyatt was struck by a sobering reality. She was as out of place here as he'd been at The Pit. She was bored senseless! He had to get her out of here before she wrote him off as a hopeless fuddy-duddy.

He paid for their drinks, let Phoebe take a couple of sips of her coffee, then took her arm. "Come on."

"We're dancing?" she asked dubiously.

"We're leaving."

Once they were outside, she gave him a bewildered look. "Aren't you enjoying yourself?"

"I was. You weren't."

"I'm having a great time," she argued.

"You almost nodded off in there. Let's just say our taste in nightclubs doesn't coincide, and do something else, okay? Do you want to stop someplace for a bite to eat?"

"Sure, I guess."

She reached for the passenger door handle, then froze, her gaze focused on something down the street. "No, wait, I have a better idea."

"Let's hear it."

"Do you like country music?"

Uh-oh. Was this more evidence of their clashing musical tastes? "Not my favorite," he admitted.

"I loathe it," she said, smiling mischievously. "There's a kicker bar down the street. Want to try it out?"

He looked where she indicated. Sure enough, there was a place called Diamonds & Studs, all lit up in neon, complete with a bucking bull that moved. "Have you lost it?"

"You felt out of place at The Pit. I felt like an alien at the jazz bar. In a kicker bar, we'll both feel like outcasts. Come on, it'll be fun."

Her infectious grin got to him. "You're on."

Phoebe insisted on paying their cover charge, since the cowboy bar was her idea. When they got inside, they found themselves in a sea of cowboy hats and pointy-toed boots, denim skirts, jeans with round impressions in the back pocket left by cans of chewing tobacco. Shirts with pearly snaps. Handlebar mustaches.

And the twangiest guitars Wyatt had ever heard.

Phoebe sauntered up to the bar. "Can we have a couple of beers?"

"Make that longnecks," Wyatt said, getting into it.

People stared. Phoebe just smiled.

They tried to line dance and failed miserably. They managed something called the Cotton-Eye Joe, but it was more like an endurance test than a dance. They both collapsed at their table when it was over, laughing hysterically. One man after another—total strangers—asked Phoebe to dance.

"Can't you see I'm with someone?" she told one man impatiently. Then she sat in Wyatt's lap.

They drank their longnecks, though Wyatt barely tasted his. He was intoxicated by Phoebe, by her sense of adventure and the way her cheeks turned pink when she felt embarrassed.

Tonight was *karaoke* night at Diamonds & Studs, and Phoebe, emboldened by her half beer, volunteered.

"You don't know any country songs," Wyatt argued.

"I'll fake it," she said. "Don't all country songs sound the same, anyway?"

She chose a song by Patsy Cline, and, as it turned out, she knew it. She had a voice like a down-and-dirty angel, and she set the place on fire.

She set Wyatt on fire, especially the way she looked at him when she sang, caressing the microphone. Mmm, mmm.

She got a standing ovation and the host asked her for an encore, but she declined. "That is the only country song I know," she said. Then she put an arm around Wyatt. "But I'll bet my friend here can do a mean Clint Black."

Wyatt nearly choked on his beer. He was as tone-deaf as a fire hydrant. "No, no thanks," he said hastily. "I think it's about time we call it a night, Miss Patsy, don't you?"

She smiled demurely. "Okay."

The minute they made it outside, they dissolved into laughter once again. "You should have seen your face," Phoebe said, "when I suggested you do Clint Black."

"You conned me! You're a closet kicker music fan!"

"No, no, it's just that I learned that one song in my voice training class."

"You sounded pretty good. Why'd you give it up?"

"I just told you, I don't know any more country songs."

"No, I mean, why'd you give up the whole acting-performing thing? You're obviously seething with talent."

She sobered. "Thank you, but it takes more than talent. You have to have ambition and persistence and connections and luck, too. I quickly found out there are lots of women with looks and talent in L.A."

He threw his arm around her shoulders. "Well, I'm just as glad you gave it up. I don't like sharing you with the world. You can sing to me anytime, though."

"A private concert, huh? That'll cost you."

"I already bought you two drinks. You're not holding out for dinner, too, are you?" he teased.

She slipped her arm around his waist and snuggled close. "Let's go home."

THEIR TASTE in nightclubs might have clashed, Phoebe mused, but their goals for the rest of the evening dovetailed perfectly. They kissed on the elevator on the way up to the third floor, and again in the hallway in front of Wyatt's front door, and again when they got inside.

Clothes fell by the wayside. They left a trail of shirts, pants and underthings from the entryway all the way to Wyatt's bedroom, stopping to kiss every few steps. By the time they reached the bed they were both gloriously nude.

Wyatt started to switch on a bedside lamp, but Phoebe stopped him. "I like it dark."

"I want to see you."

Phoebe felt inexplicably modest. As a model she'd developed a thick skin when it came to comments about her body. She'd gotten used to shedding her clothes at a moment's notice, sometimes in a communal dressing room.

But when it came to the bedroom, she was downright shy.

"Maybe next time."

"I'll hold you to it."

She was gratified to know there would *be* a next time. The more time she spent with Wyatt, the more she appreciated what he was—a strong, mature, virile man who wasn't afraid to try new things, and who wasn't afraid to admit when he'd made a mistake. He held strong opinions and had firmly drawn tastes, but there was always room for compromise.

As he tenderly pulled her with him onto the bed, her heart swelled with a new and different feeling, something unique. She hesitated to name it but it felt wonderful.

He made love to her slowly, with subtlety and finesse, qualities completely lacking in other lovers she'd had. She relished the gentle pace, letting her pleasure build slowly, without that urge to take everything as fast as she could get it because otherwise she might not get it at all. Wyatt, she knew, would never leave her wanting.

Afterward, they lay in bed for a long time, talking softly.

"I'm sure we have lots of other things in common," Wyatt said.

"You mean besides this?" She stroked his belly, then fondled him. "And a loathing for country music, of course."

"How about sports?"

"Hmm, I like swimming. And I always thought tennis would be fun."

"I like swimming. We could go to the beach."

"I like pools," she said. "The ocean scares me."

"What about hockey?"

"To play or watch?"

"Watch."

"Um, I've never tried. But I'm willing. I understand Frannie and Bill go to games. And James, Elise's fiancé, has season tickets."

"I like your friends."

Phoebe hated to end the closeness they'd achieved, but she had to. She yawned and slowly pulled herself out of Wyatt's embrace. "I have to go, you know. Before Mama sends the National Guard after me."

"You think she doesn't trust me?" Wyatt asked, all innocence.

"Would *you* trust you?"

He laughed. "No."

"She liked you," Phoebe said as she swung her legs over the side of the bed. "But then, she likes any guy who's polite, clean cut, and well dressed." She couldn't quite make herself stand up. In a total lapse of self-discipline, she draped herself over Wyatt, leaning her head against his chest. "Actually, it's a good thing she knows I've got my hooks in you. It could save you."

"From what?"

"From my mother throwing herself at you. She pretty much does that with any unattached man between thirty-five and sixty-five who has all his teeth and no prison record."

He chuckled, the low vibration tickling Phoebe's ear where it rested against his chest. "If you're so dead set against your mother's manhunting activities, maybe you should set a better example for her."

"I did *not* hunt you down. You just…happened."

"I wasn't talking about me. I'm talking about those college boys."

Phoebe stiffened. Maybe she'd misunderstood. Hadn't she already cleared up his misconception about her activities at the college? "I told you, I'm not trolling the university for a husband."

"Oh, I know. You've made your position on marriage very clear."

Was there just a tinge of disapproval in his voice? she wondered.

"But just because you're not interested in a ring," he continued, "doesn't mean you don't need companionship."

Phoebe's blood began to simmer. How dare he assume— But before she could tell him where to stick his theories about her need for *companionship*, he went on.

"You know, a mature lover has a lot more to offer than one of those college whelps."

"For instance?" she asked sharply.

"Financial stability, which means I can take you out someplace nice once in a while, instead of buying you a sub sandwich. A nice car instead of an old junker. Clearly defined expectations. And no acne or adolescent angst. I got over the abandonment issues a long time ago."

Phoebe sat up suddenly, all her warm feelings for Wyatt dissipating. He must not think much of her to believe she would weigh the pros and cons of bedding her boss versus a college classmate.

"Phoebe, what's wrong?"

"I have to go."

He sat up, too. "No, wait. I shouldn't have said all that. I was just teasing. I didn't mean to make light of what just happened. But you have to admit, we can't keep kidding ourselves. We've got something special going here, and though it might be damn inconvenient for both of us, I think we should work with it. That's all I meant."

Phoebe searched for and found her panties and dragged them on. How could she tell him it wasn't the light mood that offended her. After all, there was something a little bit funny about their predicament— wanting each other so badly they just threw aside their oh-so-soberly negotiated, nonsexual friendship.

What *did* upset her were his assumptions. She had told him flat out that she had no romantic interest in college boys, but apparently he just couldn't wrap his mind around any other reason she might head for the university every day after work.

She was just going to have to disabuse him of those notions, now, wasn't she? And she saw no better time than now. So what if he laughed at her or thought her goals preposterous? His opinion of her couldn't get much lower than it already was.

"Has it ever occurred to you to wonder what classes I'm taking at ASU?"

Chapter Twelve

Wyatt watched as Phoebe found her shirt and stretched it over her head and arms. Sensing that he wasn't going to dissuade her from dressing—or leaving—he sat up and reached for his own shirt.

"I guess I didn't think about it much," he admitted. "I figured you were taking something related to your career."

"You mean like Cosmetics 101?" She settled a piercing gaze on him that made him very uncomfortable.

"Or some kind of advanced drama classes. You were interested in acting once," he reasoned, "and I assume you enjoyed it. Even if you aren't planning to act professionally, I could see you taking classes to keep your skills sharp."

Apparently that wasn't the right answer.

He tried again. "If the truth be known, I assumed you were taking continuing education classes because you wanted something to occupy your time, and because you had a social structure at the college, a group of friends that study together or trade notes or…or…"

"Or hang out at the malt shop together?"

He was just digging himself deeper, wasn't he. "Apparently I assumed wrong?"

She said nothing as she pulled on her slacks.

"Well, if I'm so badly misinformed, it's because you've never volunteered any information. I figured if it was anything important, you'd have said something."

"I'm studying biochemistry," she said abruptly.

"What?" He burst out in nervous laughter. It sounded as if she'd said *biochemistry*.

"I'm a biochemistry major," she said, enunciating every word, "with a business minor. I have less than two years to go for my degree if I continue to carry my current class load. This semester I'm taking Organic Chemistry, Statistics, Calculus and PE. I have to carry twelve hours or I lose my scholarship."

"You have a scholarship? In bio—bio—" He couldn't believe this. Phoebe Lane, glamorous TV actress and makeup artist, wanted to be a biochemist? "Why?"

"Because I like it. Because I'm good at it. And because when I graduate, I'm going to start my own all-natural cosmetics firm, Bio-Techniques. I've already trademarked the name."

Wyatt's head was spinning. This put a whole new light on the Phoebe Lane he knew. Or the one he thought he knew.

She flipped on the light. "You look a little shell-shocked."

"That's because you just turned on the light. But I am…surprised. I mean, I think it's wonderful you have all these goals and plans, but…"

"But you can't imagine why a pretty girl like me would want to worry her pretty little head over big, bad subjects like math and science?"

"I did not say that."

"But you were thinking it."

He couldn't deny it. Yes, he was shocked. "How are you doing?"

"Well, all those big numbers are *sooooo* confusing," she said in a little-girl lisp, "and I have just a terrible time with some of the big words—"

"Phoebe…"

"I have a four-point-oh this semester. Every semester, in fact, except the last one. Physics kicked my butt."

"Four-point-oh…" he said, feeling slightly faint. He'd never in his life pulled a 4.0. And he'd majored in liberal arts, which was considerably less demanding than science and business.

Fully dressed, she sat down on the end of the bed. "Any more questions?"

"What did you make on the SAT?" he asked suspiciously.

"When I took it in high school, eight hundred or so. I don't really remember."

He felt a bit relieved. Only average. He'd made a 1240 out of 1600, which he remembered because his grandparents had been so proud at the time. He'd thought they might suggest he have the number tattooed on his forehead.

"But when I took it again a few years ago, I did considerably better. I guess I didn't try very hard in high school."

"So that means you made a…"

''Fifteen-sixty. Do you want to know about my IQ, or have you been shocked enough for one evening?''

He'd better hear it all now. ''Lay it on me.''

''One thirty-seven.''

''Oh, my God, I just made love to a genius.''

''Not quite. One-forty is considered genius level. Still, pretty good for a dumb blonde, huh?''

''I have never called you a dumb blonde,'' he said hotly.

''You thought it. Every time you used a big word, you stopped and defined it for me. You patiently explained about the political history of Russia, even though I certainly didn't ask you to. Just this evening, you lectured me on classical music. You even wondered if I understood percentages when you were explaining about the effects of light filters.''

Damn. He was guilty of all those things. ''I overexplain everything to everybody,'' he said in his own defense. ''Just ask Phyllis, or Kelly, or Kurt. I would never be attracted to a woman I didn't think was... bright.''

''Bright,'' she said, her voice brittle. ''A word normally reserved for children and dogs. Good night, Wyatt.''

''But—'' She wasn't going to listen to him, he decided. He couldn't stop her from walking out that door.

She did, without a backward glance.

Damn, he'd blown it this time. Okay, so his sweet little blond bundle of passion was a genius. He could see it. He could get used to it. Most of the women he'd dated over the years had been above-average intelligence. In fact, he was sure he would never be seriously attracted to a woman who couldn't conduct an intelligent conversation, or who never read anything more challenging than a tabloid newspaper.

He'd never, ever, thought Phoebe less than intelligent. He'd just assumed she wasn't well educated. And certainly he'd never guessed she was smarter than him.

Well, damn it, he thought, she didn't go out of her way to flaunt her braininess. She didn't use a lot of big words. She never joined in at the station when he and Phyllis got into philosophical arguments, which was frequently. And when he explained things to her, she didn't gently but firmly inform him that she already understood.

She played it just a little bit dumb, he concluded. Therefore, if he'd made a wrong assumption, he couldn't be blamed entirely for it.

He couldn't mount this ever-so-logical argument, however. Phoebe was gone, and likely not speaking to him in the near future.

Dejected, he went through the condo, picking up the trail of clothes he'd left. Maybe this was for the best. A few minutes ago he'd been ready to commit to a relationship with her. A real, monogamous, regular boyfriend-girlfriend kind of thing. Since it seemed they couldn't keep away from each other, he'd decided they might as well accept the bond growing between them instead of fighting it, which took more time and energy than giving in would have.

Phoebe would have no trouble keeping her hands off him now.

PHOEBE CREPT into her apartment. All was dark and quiet. She released a sigh, relieved her mother hadn't awakened. Maybe she'd taken a sleeping pill.

Knowing she wouldn't be able to sleep herself, Phoebe made herself some hot tea and took it onto the balcony. The night air was crisp, but she didn't care. It felt good against her overheated skin. She sat down on a deck chair, set her tea on the little wrought-iron table and proceeded to sob quietly.

Phoebe had never thought of herself as an emotional person. But when she did give in to her feelings, she did it with gusto. She figured the best way to get through this crisis with Wyatt was to wallow in it, cry it out, let it get real messy, then move on.

So she sobbed. She cried, she snuffled, she hiccuped, and she cried some more. She used up an entire box of tissue. And just when she thought she was all cried out, the balcony door opened and Olga stepped outside. She wore a satin caftan, and her hair was wrapped in a sleep turban.

"Addy? I thought I heard something out here. Are you okay?"

"I'm fine, Mama," she answered, trying to sound normal. "I just couldn't sleep."

"Baloney. That boyfriend of yours has done something to make you cry. I always know when my baby is upset." Olga came and sat on the edge of Phoebe's lounger, moving Phoebe's legs aside to accommodate her. "Tell Mama what happened."

"Wyatt isn't my boyfriend."

"Of course he is. You're not telling me you stay out until all hours of the night with some casual date, are you?"

"How do you know what time I got in?"

"Mothers have super-trained ears. You'll learn all about it when you have your own babies."

Right now, babies seemed about as far from Phoebe's reality as a trip to Pluto. She wanted babies, she realized. Daisy's plight had gotten her thinking about children in the abstract, but now she realized she really did want one or two, or a dozen. She could even see their faces. They had dark, wavy hair and gray eyes.

"Did mean ol' Wyatt Madison hurt my baby?"

Phoebe nodded miserably. Olga would worm the truth out of her one way or another.

Abruptly Olga stood and grabbed both Phoebe's hands. "Stand up."

"What? Why?" But she did as her mother requested. Olga immediately sat down in the lounger herself, then pulled Phoebe into her lap. "Mama! I'm three inches taller than you and ten pounds heavier!"

"Fifteen. I've been on a diet. Sit in my lap like a good girl. We haven't been close in so long, not since you went away to L.A."

Since Olga had her arms around Phoebe like vice clamps, she had no choice but to relax and give in to her mother's sudden spurt of maternal instinct. She laid her head on Olga's breast, just as she'd done when she was a child.

"What did he do?" Olga asked gently.

"He thinks I'm stupid."

"Nonsense. Who would think that?"

"Only everyone I meet. I got so used to projecting this ditzy blonde image when I was in Hollywood, and now, no matter what I do, people just assume I'm dumb. I thought Wyatt was different, but..."

"But what?"

"You should have seen his face when I told him I was studying biochemistry. I might as well have told him I'd joined a voodoo cult and wanted to sacrifice a chicken in his living room."

"Well, honey, I could have told you that. Men are intimidated by brainy women."

"I couldn't let him keep thinking I was hanging out at the university to pick up men."

"You could have told him you were studying home economics."

Phoebe sighed, and Olga stroked her hair. Olga just didn't get it.

"Of course, that's not what Jane Jasmine would recommend."

Phoebe sat up. "You've read the book?"

"A few chapters. I thought, if I'm going to meet the author on national television, I ought to read her book. Besides, it was just sitting on your bookshelf."

"What do you think so far?"

"Some of it makes sense, I guess. I know she's right about one thing."

"What's that?"

"No man's going to love you if you don't love yourself."

"I do love myself," Phoebe groused.

"Me, too," Olga said, without a lot of conviction.

Phoebe suspected they shared the same problem, though. They might love themselves, but they were both very, very afraid the rest of the world wouldn't. So they hid. Olga played dumb and helpless; she played the vamp; she played the carefree widow. And

Phoebe played to the blonde stereotype. She also played like she didn't want or need a man.

Nothing could have been farther from the truth.

PHOEBE WASN'T SURE how she made it through work Monday. To be sure, Wyatt stayed out of her way. If he had anything to say to her, he sent Phyllis or one of the crew. But she was very, very aware of his whereabouts all day long. And every time she saw him, it felt like an ice pick in her heart.

By the time the show was over and she was packing up to leave, she felt sick to her stomach. And she *never* got sick.

She drove to the university but skipped her last two classes, almost unheard of for her. She would have to get a copy of the lecture notes from someone later. She didn't think she would be able to focus on anything tonight, anyway.

When she got home, she found Olga in the living room surrounded by several shopping bags from Phoenix's smarter department stores. She wore what had to be a new, fashionable shorts outfit and gold, high-heeled sandals.

"Addy! You're home early."

"Not feeling too good," she said, collapsing onto the couch.

"Well, of course not. You've just had a major tiff with your honey. But I've got the cure for that."

Oh, no. Phoebe just raised her eyebrows expectantly.

"First, I bought us both sexy new bathing suits." She whipped two scraps of shiny lamé out of one of the bags.

Phoebe laughed. She couldn't help it, in the face of Olga's relentless good cheer. "Mama, you must be kidding. I'm not wearing pink lamé."

"Then you can have the blue one." She tossed the incredibly brief suit onto Phoebe's lap. "We'll take a pitcher of margaritas down to the pool and catch a few rays. But first—"

She opened another bag and pulled out several bottles and tubes. "Beauty treatments all the way around. I had this dream once that I'd come to Phoenix, and you'd get me into that ritzy spa you worked at for free."

"Are you kidding? My former boss didn't give anyone a free ride." But Phoebe was drawn to the beauty products despite herself. Just researching her future competition, she told herself. She opened up a popular brand of "miraculous moisturizer" and sniffed it. "Nothing but lanolin, lecithin, and maybe a bit of corn oil."

Olga wrinkled her nose. "You're kidding. I paid seventeen dollars for that jar."

"I could whip it up in my kitchen for about ninety-eight cents."

Olga seemed fascinated. "What about this one?" She handed Phoebe a bottle of toner. Phoebe observed the color, then sniffed. "Mostly alcohol, probably some witch hazel, stearyl ether and glycerin. And food coloring."

Olga grinned. "You're really learning something at that school of yours. Do these products even work?"

"Yeah, sure. But this one will dry out your skin," she said, holding up the toner.

"Ewww. So what do you recommend?"

Phoebe grinned, suddenly feeling a bit better. If she'd known it would be this easy to impress her mother, she'd have done it a long time ago. "Let me show you."

Twenty minutes later they both had their faces covered with Phoebe's avocado, yogurt and honey mask, and Olga was doing Phoebe's nails in a hot pink. "So what are you going to do about your producer sweetie?" Olga asked.

Phoebe sighed. "Nothing."

"Nothing! Are you sure you're my daughter? This is war, Addy. You've got to go on the offensive. Your first mission is to hang out by the pool in that swimsuit and completely ignore him."

Phoebe knew her mother's advice flew in the face of everything Jane Jasmine recommended—honesty, maturity, and no game-playing. But she had to admit, a vengeful part of her wanted to make Wyatt suffer. Proving him wrong about his assumptions would be the best revenge. But since she couldn't run out and win a Nobel Prize, she had to resort to some other method of avenging her wounded pride.

Anyway, what had Jane Jasmine done for her lately? Hiding her light under a bushel had worked just fine. But the moment she was honest with Wyatt about her abilities, her intellect and her ambitions, all hell had broken loose.

"And what's my second mission?"

Olga smiled, cracking her drying mask. "Make him jealous."

"With whom?"

"Anybody who's younger, handsomer and richer than him."

Phoebe didn't know anyone handsomer or richer. Younger, she could manage.

Well, why shouldn't she? she reasoned. Her heart was broken. She was entitled to behave like an idiot for at least one afternoon.

Phoebe blew on her nails to dry them. "Okay, Mama, you've sold me. You make up the margaritas, while my nails dry. Then we'll hit the pool and have a party."

Olga grinned, causing a big hunk of dried green glop to fall into her lap. "You *are* my daughter."

Twenty minutes later, Phoebe and Olga were parked in loungers by the pool, an ice chest between them containing a blender full of frozen margaritas. Normally Phoebe didn't sun herself. There was nothing that would age skin more rapidly than too much sun. But she couldn't exactly swim laps in the ridiculous blue lamé suit. One false move and she could be arrested for indecent exposure.

A few others had joined them—Elise and James, Daisy, Frannie, and a young married couple from the second floor who'd just moved in.

"Phoebe, that's a…an *interesting* new suit you have there," Daisy said quietly.

"My mother's idea. Don't mind me, I've gone completely around the bend."

"Does this have something to do with Wyatt?" Daisy asked perceptively.

Phoebe felt herself blushing. "I'm through with Wyatt. He thinks I'm a bimbo."

"And you're trying to prove him right?" Daisy arched an eyebrow at her.

"I'm just having a little fun. Anyway, he'll never even see this," Phoebe said, indicating the brief suit. "He'll work until midnight, like always."

"Wrong. I saw his car in the lot when I came home a while ago."

Phoebe's stomach flipped. Well, she decided, he wouldn't have any reason to come down here or even look down here. His balcony was shrouded by the big palm trees, anyway.

"Addy." Olga thumped Phoebe on the arm. "I mean, Phoebe." Olga struggled to use Phoebe's newer name when they were around others, mostly to avoid confusion. She lowered her voice to a whisper. "There aren't any single guys here. How are you going to make Wyatt jealous?"

"Easy." She nodded toward the far end of the pool, where Jeff was cleaning out one of the pool skimmers. He wore short cutoff jeans and a tank shirt, emphasizing his tan and his biceps.

"Oh, he's a cute one," Olga said almost reverently. "But not exactly rich, I'm guessing."

"Young and cute is the best I can do on short notice."

"So what are you waiting for? Go get him."

She would, after she finished her margarita, Phoebe vowed silently. She must be crazy, contemplating an open flirtation with Jeff. She might just scare him to pieces. But she had no doubt the gossip would fly. Though Wyatt wouldn't witness her flirtation himself, someone would mention it to him. The Mesa Blue grapevine was healthy.

"Wait a minute," Olga said. "Who is *that?*" She surreptitiously nodded toward the edge of the court-yard. That's when Phoebe spotted Bill, patching a crack on a concrete walkway.

"That's Bill White, our super."

"Ooh, la-la, he's a handsome devil."

"Mama, no. Don't even think about it. He's spoken for."

"Oh, nuts. Married, huh?"

"Well, no…"

Olga's eyes lit up. "Engaged?"

"Not exactly."

"Then he's fair game."

Phoebe put a hand to her forehead. There was no stopping Olga when she was like this. She only hoped the fragile state of Bill and Frannie's new romance could withstand the onslaught.

Olga straightened her bathing suit and patted her pouf of short, white-blond hair, which was almost the same shade as Phoebe's.

Phoebe drained her drink, set down her plastic tum-bler and decided to make her own move. She got up from her lounger and slunk over to where Jeff was working diligently.

"Hi, Jeff. Watcha doing?"

"Cleaning the—" He looked up, and his eyes bugged out. "Oh, hi, Phoebe. New suit?" His voice cracked slightly.

Phoebe sat down on the edge of the pool and dan-gled her feet in the water. "Yeah. Like it?"

"Oh, yeah."

"Want to join the party?"

"You want me to?" He looked at her, earnest and

a little doubtful, and Phoebe realized she couldn't trifle with his affections. Jeff was a nice kid, and his flirtations seemed meaningless, but it wouldn't be fair to encourage him under false pretenses.

"Look, Jeff, it's like this. I'm trying to make a certain guy jealous."

"You mean Wyatt?"

How was it that everyone knew there was something between her and Wyatt? She thought they'd been rather discreet.

She saw no point in denying it. "Yes."

"You mean he did something stupid like blow you off?"

It hadn't happened quite that way, Phoebe recalled with a twinge of conscience. In fact, she was the one who'd walked out. "He treated me like I was dumb," she said. "You don't think I'm dumb, do you, Jeff?"

"Hell, no, Phoebe. You're a damn rocket scientist."

Phoebe recognized a calculated line when she heard one. He probably did think she was dumb. Everybody did. When one had more than a passing resemblance to Malibu Barbie, it just came with the territory.

"So is it okay if I flirt with you? With the firm understanding I don't mean anything by it?"

Jeff's eyes lit up. "Are you kidding? It'll be great for my reputation. There are a couple of girls around here I wouldn't mind making jealous." He nodded toward the shallow end of the pool, where two college-age women were lounging, trying to be aloof. Phoebe had invited them to join the party, but they'd declined.

"Then put that skimmer back together and come get a margarita."

He frowned. "You all didn't bring glass out here, did you?"

Phoebe laughed. The pool was Jeff's true mistress. "Nope. Just plastic." She took his hand and led him back to the crowd. "Mama, pour this hardworking man a—" She realized her mother's lounger was empty.

"Over there." Daisy indicated with a nod.

Phoebe looked. Olga was chatting with Bill, and she was in full-coquette mode. "Oh, shoot," Phoebe muttered. She glanced around for Frannie but didn't see her.

"Mama!" Phoebe called, trying to distract her. But Olga didn't budge. "Olga!" she called louder. Maybe her mother was trying to pretend she didn't have a daughter Phoebe's age. Olga glanced over.

"Come meet Jeff." She linked her arm playfully in Jeff's. He grinned and slid his arm around her, enjoying his role.

Olga waved and nodded, but she wasn't budging from Bill's side. Bill, for his part, was talking and gesturing and laughing, and when Olga touched him lightly on the arm, he leaned toward her.

Bad body language, Phoebe thought. Her only consolation was that Frannie wasn't around to witness Bill's behavior. She wondered where Frannie had gone.

She got Jeff a drink herself, handed it to him, then leaned up to whisper in his ear. "Laugh like I just said something hilarious."

He laughed, then whispered back, "Now you laugh."

She did—but before she could do more, Elise and Daisy appeared on either side of her, each grabbing an elbow. They practically dragged her away.

"What do you think you're doing?" Elise said.

"Are you crazy?" Daisy asked at the same time, then added, "This is so unlike you."

"You mean that I'm acting like a complete airhead?"

"No, that you're throwing yourself at Jeff," Elise said.

"Just living up to everyone's preconceived notions," Phoebe mumbled.

"What did that brute Wyatt say to you?" Daisy asked fiercely. "Just say the word, and I'll beat him up."

The picture of petite, feminine Daisy going toe-to-toe with six-foot-one Wyatt made Phoebe smile. "Nothing much. He just laughed at my dreams and couldn't believe I was smart enough to be a scientist."

"The ogre," Elise muttered.

"Okay, so he's a miserable cockroach," Daisy said. "What are you trying to accomplish here?"

Phoebe sighed. "Maybe I'm just tired of fighting who and what I am. I'm sick of downplaying my looks and trying to get people to respect me for my brain."

Elise and Daisy looked at each other, obviously perplexed, then back at Phoebe. "Phoebe, dear," Elise said. "I don't know how to break this to you, but you've never tried to impress anyone with your brain. *We* know you're smart. But you do tend to downplay that side of yourself."

"Hah. You should have heard me at Wyatt's last night. I told him my GPA, my SAT scores, even my IQ. I didn't hide any smarts under any bushel. I did just what Jane Jasmine advises—and Wyatt laughed at me."

Elise and Phoebe looked at each other again.

"What kind of numbers are we talking about, here?" Daisy asked cautiously.

Phoebe realized she'd never told her best friends the whole truth. They knew she was going to school, they knew she was studying biochemistry. But that was the most she'd told them. So she spilled it. Everything. And when she was done, they just stared.

"You're a genius?" her friends said together.

"See?" Phoebe cried, thoroughly frustrated.

"See what? You probably scared the poor man to death," Elise said. "Yes, men like smart women. But Jane Jasmine aside, I can see how a man, any man, might be a little frightened by a woman with enough IQ for two people."

"You scared us," Daisy added. "And before you get all defensive, it's not just because you're blond and pretty. I'd be surprised if Jeff or Frannie or *anyone* I thought I knew suddenly revealed a hidden side of him- or herself."

"Wyatt was probably just surprised," Elise said. "He'll get used to it."

No, he won't, Phoebe thought, because she wasn't going to give him the chance. She'd been insane to allow anything to develop between them. He would never be able to think of her as anything but a former-actress-turned-makeup-artist.

"Maybe so," Phoebe said noncommittally. "But meanwhile, I'm having fun. Jeff and I are just kidding around. He thought having a TV star on his arm might impress those snotty coeds. So just let us have our fun, okay?"

Elise and Daisy sighed together. "Okay," Elise said, "but be careful. Don't shoot yourself in the foot."

Chapter Thirteen

It was all Wyatt could do to fix himself a bologna sandwich for dinner. Today's show hadn't gone very well—too much boring chitchat, not enough happening. Kelly and Kurt weren't speaking to each other— again. And Phoebe wasn't speaking to Wyatt. The tension on the set had been thick enough to churn.

He took his sandwich and headed out to the balcony to catch the last of the day's warmth before the desert cool set in. That was something he was still getting used to in Phoenix. It could be a hundred degrees during the day, even in April, but at night it got downright cold.

As he set his plate on the patio table, he made a quick visual check of Helen's plants to make sure all were thriving. His gaze fell on the cactus, the one that had jabbed Phoebe and sent her flying into his arms.

It wasn't blooming. He'd been sweet-talking it for weeks, despite how foolish it made him feel to converse with a plant. And still no blooms.

The sound of guitar music drew him to the railing. Someone was having a party down by the pool. He peered through the fronds of the concealing palm tree and caught a glimpse of a small group—then his eyes bugged out. He saw not one, but two platinum blondes. One of them was Phoebe, and she wasn't wearing that conservative tank suit she usually wore to swim laps. This suit was shiny and blue—and skimpy.

A wave of jealousy washed over him. She'd sure never worn that suit in front of him.

The wave resolved itself into a tyrannosaurus rex chewing on his insides when he saw Phoebe sit beside Jeff, the pool guy, and casually drape an arm around him. It certainly hadn't taken her long to find a replacement, he thought uncharitably.

Would she sleep with him tonight? The thought made Wyatt so furious he wanted to climb down the palm tree, charge into the midst of that party and throttle Jeff until his teeth rattled. But that was hardly fair to Jeff. He was a victim, just as Wyatt had been.

He glanced back at the cactus, sitting there all innocent-like. Mocking him and his obsession.

"To hell with you, stupid cactus! Just *don't* bloom. See if I care!"

"Halloo up there!"

Startled, Wyatt thought for one panicked moment that the cactus was talking back. When the greeting was repeated, he looked around, then down at the source of the voice. He could just see Frannie on her patio, waving at him. Normally she wouldn't have been able to spot him, but he'd been leaning so far over the railing trying to get a better view of Phoebe that Frannie couldn't have helped but notice him.

"Hi, Frannie," he called back.

"You want to have our own party?"

"Pardon me?"

"I figured since those Jersey blondes were ruining both our love lives, we could hang out together. Misery loves company."

Jersey blondes?

"Come on down. I'll put on a pot of coffee."

She disappeared before he could tell her he didn't drink coffee. He decided he'd better go down there and explain that *his* misery didn't need any company, thanks very much. But if she needed a shoulder to cry on, he supposed he could oblige. Frannie was a very nice woman and a very good friend of his grandparents.

He finished his sandwich on the way downstairs.

Frannie greeted him at the door still in her swimsuit, but she'd thrown a matching long skirt over it. Apparently she'd been at the pool party and had chosen to abandon the festivities. But she wasn't wearing her usual cheery smile.

"I don't drink coffee," he said by way of greeting.

"Oh, that's right, you're the orange juice kid. I'll get you some."

"That's really not—"

But she'd already flown into the kitchen. Her movements reflected a kind of quiet desperation.

One of her cats, a small calico, wrapped itself around Wyatt's ankles. Absently he picked it up and scratched its head. The cat purred contentedly in his arms. Too bad women weren't this easy, he mused grimly. He couldn't just scratch Phoebe on the head and expect her to be happy. She also expected him to read her mind and to not even blink when she suddenly revealed her head was full of physics and higher math instead of lipstick shades.

Frannie returned with a big glass of orange juice. "So what happened with you and Phoebe?" she asked point-blank. "Why is she out there flirting with Jeff when you're up in your apartment alone?" She led him into the dining room, shooed a cat off a chair, and offered the seat to him.

He wished he had an easy answer. "She had expectations of me which I failed to meet," he said diplomatically. "I didn't show appropriate respect for her life goals."

"Wyatt. You made fun of her goals? What goals does Phoebe have, anyway? Does she want to get back into television or something?" Frannie got out a pack of playing cards and absently shuffled them.

"She wants to be a biochemist."

Frannie laughed.

"See?"

She immediately sobered. "You mean, really?"

"Uh-huh. What's your story?"

Frannie's face scrunched into a scowl. "It's Blondie's mother, Olga. She doesn't look like anybody's mother."

Wyatt silently agreed. Moms ought to look like— well, more like Frannie.

"She didn't waste ten minutes getting her hooks into Bill, and it was all over but the crying."

"Bill chose her over you? I don't believe that."

"It's true. And why couldn't you believe it? She's thin and gorgeous, just like Phoebe—and does she flirt! 'Oh, Bill, that's so clever how you're mending that crack in the sidewalk,'" she said in a flawless imitation of Olga's peculiar Danish-Jersey accent. "She did everything Jane Jasmine said not to, and it worked like a charm. Bill was all over her."

"I'm sure he was just being polite."

"Laughing like a hyena at her jokes and adjusting her swimsuit strap for her is more than polite."

"Ah."

"There's only one thing to do," Frannie said.

"What?" Wyatt had to admit he was so desperate at this point he would cling to any strategy Frannie could think of.

"Do you know how to play canasta?"

"WHAT HAPPENED to Frannie?" Phoebe asked, when she finally was able to get Bill alone.

Bill looked around the crowd, which was starting to thin now that evening had set in. "Gee, I don't know. Haven't seen her in a while. She probably went to feed her cats or something."

Phoebe doubted that. Bill hadn't taken his eyes off Olga all evening. Such behavior was bound to be noticed.

"Maybe I should go look for her."

"That's a great—"

"Oh, Bill, there you are," Olga said, sauntering over with yet another drink in her hand. She'd had way too much.

"I noticed another crack in the sidewalk," Olga said. "Maybe you should fix it while you've got your tools out. I just love watching a man work."

Bill's eyes lit up. "I'll just do that."

Phoebe sighed. Maybe she'd better go find Frannie and see what was up. She packed up the ice chest,

said her good-nights and went upstairs. Then she
threw on a long T-shirt over her suit and headed back
down.

"Come in," Frannie called cheerily, when Phoebe
knocked.

Phoebe entered. Frannie didn't sound upset. That
was good. She found Frannie in the dining room playing cards. With Wyatt.

"Oh, it's you," Frannie said, sounding supremely
disappointed. She threw down her cards in disgust.
"Oh, Phoebe, how could you?"

"How could I what?"

"Invite that she-devil mother of yours into our
home, then throw her at my Bill! After I worked so
hard to get him!"

"But my mother's only here for—" Phoebe saved
her breath. Frannie ran from the room sobbing. Three
cats trotted after her down the hall. A door slammed.

"Well, that didn't go too well," Wyatt said.
"Sounds like the Jersey Blondes are breaking hearts
all over the place. What happened to Jeff?"

Jersey Blondes? "He threw me over for someone
younger."

"Lot of that going around."

"Oh, Wyatt, I am not interested in Jeff," she felt
compelled to say. She wasn't into playing games, no
matter what her mother advised.

"Could have fooled me."

So, he'd seen her performance, despite the fact that
he'd never joined the party. "You were spying on me
from your balcony," she concluded.

"You were cavorting in public for all the world to

see. I could hardly help noticing your behavior—or your new swimsuit.''

"I was humoring my mother. She bought it for me.''

"That figures.''

Phoebe instantly felt protective. "Don't say bad things about my mother. She's very sweet, just a little misguided.''

"Sounds like she's a home-wrecker.''

"Bill and Frannie aren't married. And let's not forget, Bill had a hand in this. He could have discouraged my mother, but he didn't.''

"She looks like you, so who could blame him?''

Phoebe wasn't certain if she was being complimented or insulted. But the next moment she realized it was the latter.

"How do you and your mother manage to get your hair exactly the same shade? It's uncanny.''

"I'll have you know, I'm a natural blonde!''

"How could I know that? You wouldn't let me turn the lights on.''

"Ohh!'' She was so startled by his rudeness that that was all she could manage for a few moments. Finally she summoned the wherewithal to leave. "I hope you and Frannie have a wonderful evening together!'' She slammed the door behind her.

"MAMA, DON'T SCRUNCH UP your face like that,'' Phoebe said. "You'll end up with white creases.''

"I can't help it,'' Olga said, trying to relax her face as Phoebe applied foundation to it. "And I think you might have just accused me of having wrinkles.''

They were in a guest dressing room on the "Heads

Up'' set. As if Phoebe weren't cranky enough, given how her life had been going lately, she had to make up a total of eight women this morning—and the first, Olga, had a ticklish face.

Everybody was mad at her. Neither Wyatt nor Frannie would talk to her. Elise and Daisy didn't exactly shun her, but they weren't behaving like the most loyal of friends. They blamed her for throwing away what she had with Wyatt, and every time either of them tried to talk to her about it, she ended up just changing the subject because she couldn't make them understand how deeply Wyatt's ridicule had cut her.

Her mother was talking to her, but barely. They'd had a huge fight the night after the pool party. Olga had painstakingly explained that she hadn't realized Bill's girlfriend was Frannie, that neither Frannie nor Bill had given her the slightest indication they were together, so she hadn't seen the harm. Bill had made her feel feminine and desirable, even if the flirtation hadn't gone anywhere.

Phoebe had responded by telling Olga she would be Jane Jasmine's most spectacular failure. She'd immediately apologized, but Olga's feelings had been hurt. They'd been walking on eggshells around each other ever since.

Even she and Richie had argued. She'd forgotten she was supposed to take notes yesterday for a class Richie had to miss, and she'd skipped it.

Frannie and Bill also weren't speaking to each other.

Even Kelly and Kurt weren't talking, which had nothing to do with Phoebe, except she was beginning to feel like her entire life was a minefield.

Olga giggled, causing Phoebe to smear her eye-liner. "Mama!"

"Sorry, sweetie. I can't help it. Remember when you were little and I used to make up your face for dress-up? You used to giggle and say it tickled."

"I was five years old." She blotted away the mistake and started over. "Those were fun times, though," she admitted, grasping the olive branch Olga had extended. Her mother had instilled in her a love for cosmetics, grooming and pretty clothes. She still loved all those things. But her attraction to such frivolities had caused people to assume her head was empty of anything weightier.

Phoebe finished with Olga and sent her to the Green Room to wait. A seemingly endless stream of women followed. Phoebe found herself trying to guess which ones were the ones who'd succeeded in finding Mr. Right, and which ones were still looking. By her sixth makeup job, she'd figured it out. The ones who'd found mates weren't the prettiest or the thinnest or the youngest. They were the ones who carried themselves with a quiet confidence. Their smiles were genuine, and they didn't express concern about whether the TV camera would add ten pounds.

They liked themselves, and they didn't give a rat's ears what anybody else thought of them. One of them mentioned she worked in nuclear medicine. She was no dummy, and she didn't hide the fact. In fact, she wore horn-rimmed glasses that made her look like a librarian. Yet she was quite attractive in her own way. It was her smile, and the twinkle in her eye.

"Oh, my, you've made me look like a movie star!"

the woman exclaimed when she regarded the final results in the mirror.

"The studio lights will tone it down some."

"I wasn't complaining. My fiancé will be in the audience, and I can't wait for him to see me like this!"

Phoebe's final pre-on-air task was to do Jane Jasmine's makeup. She looked much as she did in the publicity picture printed on the back cover of *2001 Ways to Wed.* She was about forty-five, Phoebe guessed, and she wore her dark hair in a no-nonsense, short and curly style. Her skin was flawless but her features were too sharp for her to be considered a classic beauty. She even had a few gray hairs, which she didn't bother to color.

"I'm not sure whether I should shake your hand or punch you out," Phoebe joked as she settled Jane into the chair and tied a smock over her.

"Oh?"

"One of my best friends is engaged because of your book. My other best friend is alone and completely miserable, despite having dutifully followed your advice."

Jane was immediately sympathetic. "Results sometimes take a while. Do you want me to talk to her?"

Phoebe shook her head. "I tried to get her on the show, but she wouldn't do it."

"So how about you?" Jane asked. "Did you read the book?"

"Cover to cover. Just for my friend, though."

Jane nodded wisely. "Not looking for a husband yourself, huh?"

"No. But then this man came along—"

"—when you least expected one. I'll bet you were quietly going about your business, engrossed in your own highly interesting, well-directed life, and there he was."

"Well, yes."

"That is precisely my primary message. Men flock around when you work on yourself as a person, when you focus on your own goals and dreams." Jane smiled. "Although, I'm guessing you've never had a problem with men not flocking."

"Don't smile, please.... Oh, I manage to scare them off one way or another, but usually it's intentional."

"Not this time?"

Phoebe shook her head, fighting back the sting of tears. "First off, he saw your book on my shelf and assumed I was husband-hunting."

"Uh-oh."

"We got over that, finally, but then I got up the nerve to open up to him and share my dreams and goals, and, well, it was just awful. He laughed."

"What kind of dreams and goals?" Jane asked.

Phoebe was still nervous when it came to honesty about her career aspirations. But she forced herself to say it. "I'm going to become a biochemist and start my own cosmetics company."

"Oh, that's marvelous! But I know why the guy laughed."

"Because he thinks I'm dumb?"

"Because you surprised him, that's all. You'd better get used to the fact that no one thinks of a beautiful, blond TV star when you say 'biochemist.' You also made him nervous, honey. Your looks are intimidating enough. Combine that with brains, and you're one scary package. The man would have to have quite a strong sense of self-esteem to stand up to that.''

"Wyatt doesn't lack self-esteem," Phoebe murmured.

"You mean Wyatt Madison? The producer?"

Phoebe wanted to sew her lips shut. "Yes."

"You're in love with him?" Jane asked gently.

Phoebe nodded. She did love Wyatt, and she had for a long time. She just hadn't wanted to admit it to herself.

"So what did you do when he laughed?"

Jane seemed fascinated with the whole thing—like an avid biologist dissecting a frog. And Phoebe found herself wanting to spill her guts. She supposed that was what made Jane a good therapist.

"I got mad. And I left. And I... It sounds so stupid now. I put on a blue lamé swimsuit and flirted with a twenty-two-year-old."

To her credit, Jane didn't criticize.

"And what did Wyatt do?"

"He got mad, too."

"Uh-huh."

"And he thought I bleached my hair."

Jane gasped. "The wretch. Forget him. I'm sure there are lots of men out there who would assume, without you telling them, that you're a natural blond."

Phoebe had to laugh at herself. "It was the way he said it, but never mind."

"Honey, if he laughed at you, it was because you've been hiding your intellect from him, so your announcement surprised him, that's all. You're the one who didn't make him understand. Sit him down and calmly *make* him understand who you really are. If he can't love that person, then fine, you gave it your best shot. But don't throw a good thing out the window just because he reacted badly the first time you let him see what was behind those pretty blue eyes."

Phoebe was silent after that, digesting what Jane had said. Maybe she'd overreacted to Wyatt's less-than-perfect behavior. Maybe, she thought, she'd deliberately let the budding relationship self-destruct. Because maybe, deep down, she didn't feel worthy of a man like Wyatt.

WYATT WATCHED his show unfold like an orchid— or maybe a Venus flytrap, he amended. This was certainly the most sensational show he'd ever done— leaning toward Jerry Springer. He'd vowed he would never resort to melodrama or faked fistfights to attract viewers, but the conflict evolving on the set was all too real. Riveting, but it made him uncomfortable.

Uncomfortable especially because he could see Phoebe on the opposite side of the stage, watching intently. She was concerned about her mother, he realized, as well she should be. Jane Jasmine did not pull her punches.

"You're afraid of something, Olga," Jane said. "I can tell by the colors you wear, the way you hold yourself, even the way you smile. You're hiding the real Olga Phelps. You are so afraid of someone seeing the real you that you have to hide behind this glamorous persona. You have no trouble getting a first date, I bet."

"No, none at all," Olga said with a brittle smile.

"But after one or two dates the guys disappear into the woodwork."

Olga's smile faded. "After they get to know me, I guess."

"No, that's not it. They *can't* get to know you because you don't let them. They try to crack through your veneer, and you probably turn the conversation right back to the man."

"You say in your book to show an interest in the man's work," Olga said defensively.

"I said cultivate an interest. Learn about it so you can have meaningful conversations. That doesn't mean constantly stroking his ego and treating your own goals and interests as insignificant."

Olga suddenly burst into tears. "But I don't *have* any goals and interests. Except to get married. That's all I've ever wanted."

Jane reached out and squeezed Olga's hand. "We're going to work on that."

Wyatt kept his gaze on Phoebe. She had one hand over her mouth and the other tightly wrapped around herself, as if she had to physically restrain herself from coming to her mother's rescue.

"What do you like to do," Jane asked, "that has nothing to do with men?"

"Well," Olga said in a halting voice, "I make wreaths. I brought one with me today, but the producer wouldn't let me bring it on."

Kelly interrupted. "Let's have a look at this wreath!"

"After this commercial break," Kurt put in. He and Kelly had started holding hands during one of

Jane's mini-counseling sessions. Wyatt suspected something she'd said had resonated with them.

They cut to commercial, and Kelly immediately let him have it. "Wyatt! Why didn't you let Phoebe's nice mother bring her wreath onto the show?"

Wyatt threw up his hands. "Fine. Never mind that it has nothing to do with anything we're talking about. Bring on the wreath."

He turned away and bumped right into Phoebe.

"Sorry," they said together. Then they just looked at each other for a long, searing moment.

"Phoebe!" Phyllis called. "We need touch-ups."

With a nod to Wyatt, she scurried onto the set, powder and brush in hand. He thought she'd been about to say something to him, and he wondered what that was.

Wyatt fetched the wreath, giving it a closer look on the way back to the set. Olga had made it for Phoebe, he realized. It held a dozen or more tiny mementos of Phoebe's life—all related to her TV career. Apparently Wyatt wasn't the only one to have pigeonholed Phoebe.

"Fifteen seconds," the director announced. The set buzzed with frenetic activity, then the cameras rolled again.

"I made it for my daughter," Olga explained, when Jane asked about the wreath. "She played Vanessa Vance on 'Skin Deep,' if you remember that show."

"And she's backstage," Kelly said, practically bubbling over. "Can we bring her on?"

The audience clapped. A few of the men whistled and made catcalls.

Wyatt died a thousand horrible deaths. His show was veering off course like a sailboat in a hurricane. He was going to throttle Kelly—she knew better than to stray from the script. And Phoebe... Where was Phoebe, anyway?

She had disappeared.

Chapter Fourteen

Phoebe made a beeline for the dressing rooms. There was no way she was going on camera, not with braided hair and a shiny nose. Hell, not even if she'd just walked out of a salon. She wasn't going in front of a TV camera unless it was to announce the launch of Bio-Techniques.

Someone called her name, and she walked faster, pretending not to hear—until she realized the voice didn't belong to anyone on the crew. She skidded to a stop and turned around to find the last person she expected to see backstage.

"Elise?"

Elise caught up with her. She wore a visitor's badge and carried a rolled-up paper sack. "Where are you running off to?"

"Anywhere but in front of those cameras. They were trying to put me on the show. What are you doing here?" She took Elise's elbow and steered her into Kelly's dressing room. No one would think to look for her here. She tried not to look at the white fur rug.

"Wow, this is kind of a weird room," Elise said,

gazing around at the red walls imprinted with huge, purple lips.

"It belongs to Kelly, our hostess. She's a bit of an eccentric, but very sweet. Have a seat. Oh, unless you want to watch the show from backstage."

"I can do that some other time," Elise said, settling onto the white sofa. "What's up with you? Why are you so freaked out about the idea of going on camera? I would think you'd be immune to stage fright by now."

"It's not stage fright. But that part of my life is over—the Vanessa Vance part. I just wish everyone would forget it."

"Are you ashamed of the work you did on that show?"

"Yes," she answered without hesitation.

"I don't know why. Lots of great actors got their start on soap operas and TV commercials."

"But I don't want to be an actor."

Elise gave her a sage look. "Kiddo, I think you're taking this much too seriously. You are not the only person in the world to make a career misstep. For my first summer job I answered the phone at an illegal escort service."

"No way."

"It's true. I didn't have a clue what was going on until the vice squad raided the place. I had to call my parents from jail."

"That's so sordid!"

"It is, but I can laugh about it now. Stop taking yourself so seriously. Life is pretty hysterical most of the time, and if you can't laugh about the twists and turns you might as well join a cloistered convent in Tibet and give it all up.''

Phoebe did crack a smile. Elise was so wise. ''What's in the bag?''

''Oh. Something *really* important.'' She opened the sack and pulled out several fabric swatches. ''I really came by to show you these and get your advice. I thought maybe we could grab lunch on our way to campus. You have a twelve-thirty class, right?''

''Yes, but I have to take Mama home first, so I won't have time for lunch. Sorry.'' She examined the lush fabrics—satins, brocades, lace; some in white, some in ivory. Elise had settled on a traditional design with a fitted bodice, puff sleeves and a gently flounced skirt with a train.

''This plain ivory satin is gorgeous,'' Phoebe said, unable to disguise the longing in her voice. ''The brocade and the lace are too busy—they would compete with the beautiful details of the gown. This satin will move beautifully with you and give a softer look to the dress.''

''You don't think plain satin is too, well, plain?''

''Maybe some scalloped lace at the hem and neckline. Well, I'm sure your dressmaker can handle those details.''

''I knew you would have the answer,'' Elise said. ''I can't wait to see what sort of wedding dress you choose for yourself.''

''Hah! At the rate I'm going, I'll get married about the same time I draw Social Security. You'll be pushing me down the aisle in a wheelchair.''

''So you haven't patched things up with Wyatt, huh?''

"No."

"Are you going to try?"

Phoebe sighed. "I don't know that I'm ready for a relationship with a man like Wyatt."

"Maybe not, but what if, when you finally do feel ready, no guys are available? Think about Daisy's predicament."

"I wish I could give Wyatt to Daisy."

"Oh, you do not. If Daisy showed the slightest interest in Wyatt, you'd scratch her eyes out."

Phoebe grinned. "You're right, I would."

"Hey, do you think I could meet Jane Jasmine? I'd like to thank her in person for helping me find James."

"Go talk to Wyatt. He'll introduce you. I'm going to hide out back here a few minutes longer."

"Scaredy-cat."

"Yup."

WYATT BREATHED a huge sigh of relief when the closing credits rolled. The show had gotten back on track, thanks to Jane's smooth segue into the next guest's problems finding a man.

Someone tapped his arm, and for a fleeting half-second he hoped it was Phoebe. But it was Elise Foster, of all people.

"Hi, Wyatt," she whispered, since the cameras were still rolling. "Phoebe said you might introduce me to Jane Jasmine."

He nodded. "Sure." As Phyllis pumped the audience for that last little bit of applause, Wyatt led Elise toward the stage. "Don't trip on those cords. I'll introduce you to Jane if you tell me where Phoebe's hiding.''

"And…CUT!" Phyllis bellowed. "Great job, everybody."

The applause died down and the studio suddenly buzzed with conversation and activity.

Elise smiled. "Kelly's dressing room. But don't tell her I gave her away."

Jane already had a crowd around her. Wyatt grabbed Phyllis as she passed. "This is Elise. Will you make sure she gets a private introduction to Jane Jasmine?"

Phyllis smiled. "No problem. Hi, Elise."

The two women struck up a conversation, and Wyatt made his escape. If he didn't hurry, Phoebe would slip out a side door—and he would have to track her down at home. He'd do that if he had to, but he preferred not to delay their confrontation. If he didn't say what was on his mind now, he might never get up the nerve again.

He found her without too much trouble, probably because she figured no one would look there. She sat cross-legged on the sofa hugging a pillow, and when Wyatt walked in without knocking, she shot him a look that might have vaporized a less determined man.

"That was rotten of Kelly to try to drag me on stage without asking first, and I stand firmly behind my decision to run like a scalded cat."

Wyatt chuckled. "And I firmly support your right to do so. I will speak with Kelly again about deviating from the script."

Phoebe seemed to relax a little, now that she knew that matter was settled.

Wyatt sat on the opposite end of the sofa, not too close. "Want to talk about what else is bothering you?"

"Wyatt, I can't work here anymore."

"What?" That wasn't what he'd expected to hear. He'd thought she might rant and rave a little. Yell at him. Put him in his place. He certainly hadn't anticipated her resignation.

"I can probably get my job back at the spa. I thought I could handle this, but it's too close to the life I left behind in L.A. And I left it behind for a reason."

"What reason?"

"I didn't like myself very much when I was an actress. I slept my way into that role as Vanessa Vance. Oh, I guess I cared something for the guy. I even thought I loved him. But he told me, when we broke up, that the only reason he gave me the part of Vanessa was because I was good in bed."

Wyatt winced. He didn't like hearing this. Of course he'd known Phoebe had experience, but he didn't want to hear a blow-by-blow.

"There were other times, too, when I was intimate with someone I shouldn't have been. Sometimes it was just easier not to fight the tidal wave."

"You don't have to tell me this."

"I want to. There are lots of things I should have told you before now. But I think it's too late."

He wanted to argue with her. He wanted to hold her in his arms, comfort her. She was so achingly beautiful, even with her hair in braids. But he didn't do anything except sit there because he was too afraid of mangling things even worse than they already were.

"So, you misspent your youth. A lot of people do that. Does that really mean you can't work on the show? I need you."

"I can't work so close to you. It hurts."

"It only hurts because we're not together."

"We can't be together."

"Why not?" He barely whispered the words.

"Because…because you'll never see me as anything but—"

"Bull. I see what you show me. Try again, because that's a cop-out."

"Because I'm not ready to let anybody love me. It's like Jane says—I have to work on myself first."

They'd never talked about love, but the moment she said the word, Wyatt knew it was there, glittering between them, tempting but somehow forbidden.

"When will you be ready? When you've got your college degree? When you start your business? When you make a million dollars? When?"

"I don't know."

"Well, while you're figuring that out, you can also chew on this. I love you, Phoebe. I don't care what your IQ is, or whether you have a college degree, or how many men you've slept with, or what size bra you wear, or even whether you're called Phoebe or Adelaide. I love the essence of you.

"So you think about it, and you just let me know when you're ready for a real man to love you. And if the answer is never, then congratulations. You're destined for a long and very lonely life."

He left before he said anything else. He hadn't meant to be so hard on her. But if he hadn't forcefully stated his case, she would have slipped right through his fingers.

She might, anyway.

"I DIDN'T KNOW you would be so sensitive about it," Olga said, sitting in the passenger seat of Phoebe's car on their way home from the show. "I'm proud of you and I just wanted to show you off."

"You're proud of who I used to be."

"No, that's not it. I'm proud of everything you've done and all you've turned out to be. I'm very excited about your cosmetics company. I just didn't understand, before, what a big deal this science stuff is for you."

Phoebe smiled. "Thank you, Mama."

"I think I understand a little better now why it's so important to have a career or a hobby or a cause. I used to think those were things a woman did when she couldn't find a man."

"Or as an excuse for keeping men at arm's length," Phoebe murmured.

"What?"

"Nothing. Go on."

"I never realized that taking care of your own spiritual and intellectual needs would actually make you *more* attractive."

"You sound like a true convert."

"Listening to those other women—the happy ones with boyfriends and husbands—convinced me. Jane convinced me."

"That Jane is a pretty smart lady." Phoebe pulled

her car up in front of Mesa Blue. "I should be home from class around four. We can go out for dinner or something before I have to take you to the airport."

"Okay." Olga hugged her. "You go study hard. I want to see straight *A*s on that report card, young lady."

Phoebe tried not to laugh. Olga had never cared a whit what grades Phoebe made in school.

Richie was waiting for her with a sub sandwich, when Phoebe arrived at the university.

"I thought you were mad at me," she said, as they settled onto the library steps to eat lunch.

"I got over it. It'd be pretty stupid to stay mad at you when you're the only reason I'm passing this class." He tugged on one of her braids and smiled.

Yeah, it was stupid to stay mad, she decided. Wyatt had left the door open. He'd said he loved her, something she'd tucked away in her heart for further study—later, when she had a moment of quiet time. All she had to do now was walk through that door.

But she couldn't do it halfway. Wyatt wanted all of her, body and soul, warts and all. If she wasn't prepared to put it all on the line for him, she might as well not bother.

WHEN PHOEBE GOT HOME later that day, the first thing she noticed was that Olga's wreath was back on the door. But there was something different about it. Olga had added a few things—a tiny test tube, a miniature textbook with *Biochemistry* painted on the cover, an Arizona State University lapel pin and the smallest cosmetics tube Phoebe had ever seen, labeled, Phoebe's Green Mask.

Phoebe laughed out loud even as the thoughtful gesture brought tears to her eyes. How had her mother ever come up with those things on such short notice?

When she entered her apartment, she got another surprise. She heard two women laughing in the kitchen, and when she followed the laughter she found Olga and Frannie kneading dough together.

"Frannie?" Phoebe said in surprise.

"Oh, Phoebe, your mother is so funny. Do you know what she just said? She just said—"

"I thought she was 'that Jersey Blonde'!"

"That was before I saw her on 'Heads Up' this morning. Oh, my gosh, she is so much like me it's uncanny. All those things she was saying—it could have been me. And I knew exactly where she was coming from—"

"And I wasn't going to go home without apologizing to your friend," Olga cut in. "I didn't mean to break up her romance with Bill."

"Olga's showing me how to make authentic Danish. As if my waistline needs it!"

Olga waved a finger at Frannie. "Uh-uh-uh, no cutting yourself down. Remember what Jane says. We have to stop worrying about being perfect and love ourselves just the way we are."

"Oh, you're so right."

"Did you patch things up with Bill?" Phoebe asked Frannie.

"No, and he can just forget it. He's obviously much too fickle. He doesn't deserve a catch like me, and, anyway, I'm no longer interested," Frannie said, nose in the air. "I have many important things to do to fulfill myself."

Jane Jasmine has created a couple of monsters! Phoebe was about to make her escape from the *Twilight Zone* kitchen, but Olga stopped her.

"Phoebe, you look tired. Why don't you take a little nap? We don't have to go out to dinner."

"No, I want to take you someplace nice on your last evening," Phoebe insisted. "But I wouldn't mind taking a quick swim." That would rejuvenate her better than a nap would.

She passed up the blue lamé and put on one of her nice, safe tank suits, grabbed a towel and headed for the pool.

Nothing cleared her head like swimming laps. As her muscles went through the automatic motions, pulling her gently through the water, her mind worked things over of their own accord.

Wyatt loved her. And she loved him. Oh, how she loved him. He was a good man, intelligent, kind, funny. She'd been afraid to let herself even be attracted to him, much less fall in love. She'd tossed out every obstacle to a serious relationship she could think of, because she'd sensed that there would be no turning back once it happened.

And she'd been right.

Could they make it work? Did she dare even hope…?

Well, damn it, why not? She was a perfectly good match for Wyatt, even if she was younger than him. Jane Jasmine said age didn't really matter as long as…good gravy, now *she* was quoting Jane Jasmine. Maybe all the women living in Mesa Blue should start a Jasmine cult.

That made her laugh, which caused her to inhale a

mouthful of water. Her head shot up and she grasped the nearest edge, coughing and sputtering.

"You okay?" Wyatt asked, sounding worried. His abrupt appearance only startled her, causing her to cough some more, but she nodded.

"Yes, I think I'll live."

He handed her a towel. "I knew I was quite a catch, but I'm not worth drowning yourself over."

WHAT WAS WYATT DOING hanging out at the pool? Phoebe wondered as she completed her coughing performance. She vaulted out of the pool, sat on the edge and dried her face and shoulders.

She finally steeled herself to look up at him. He wore a pair of very brief swim trunks—and nothing else. She realized she'd never seen his body in full sunlight before. It took her breath away. He might be pushing forty, but he was in better shape than most young men half his age.

"I didn't know you like to swim," she said, because she couldn't think of anything else.

"There are lots of things you don't know about me, because I've been a workaholic ever since I moved to Phoenix." Wyatt sat on the edge of the pool next to Phoebe. "I'm going to change that. Jane Jasmine says you have to strike a balance between career and personal life."

"Another Jane Jasmine devotee?"

"She's got something. Besides, if I'm expecting you to slow down enough to have a relationship, I'll have to do the same."

"You're not going to let me off the hook, here, are you?"

"No. And I don't want to hear that you're still working on yourself. Since you left L.A., you've had several years of working on yourself. You ought to be damn near perfect by now."

"Oh, Wyatt, we both know that's not true."

"Okay, you're not perfect. Neither am I. We'll work on it. We'll make mistakes and learn from them. We'll fight and we'll make up, and maybe by the time we're my grandparents' age we'll have it all figured out."

Phoebe opened her eyes wide. "What are you saying?"

"I'm saying I was an idiot for ever thinking a no-strings affair would be good enough for you, for us. We deserve something a little more…settled."

Phoebe had one card left. She had one more obstacle she could throw between them. She knew Wyatt was marriage-shy. He'd freaked out when he thought he was quarry for her husband hunt. But she knew now that the only way she was going to have Wyatt in her life was if she got the whole enchilada. No more half measures. Both of them needed the security of commitment. Besides, she *deserved* that kind of relationship.

She closed her eyes and said the words she knew might drive him away. "If you're planning on monopolizing my time until we're in our eighties, I expect a marriage license."

"Well, what the hell else do you think I meant? Open your eyes, Phoebe."

She did, and right in front of her nose was the loveliest square diamond solitaire, along with a band holding a row of tiny diamonds.

"I want you to be my wife."

She clasped both hands over her mouth, so overcome she couldn't speak. Her eyes filled with tears, and she started trembling.

"A simple yes or no would be very helpful."

She nodded yes.

He pried her left hand away from her face and slipped the ring onto her third finger. "It belonged to my mother. I was too young when she died to remember much about her, but my grandmother says she was the most loving, generous and happy person they'd ever met."

Phoebe finally found her voice. "I don't de—"

"Don't you dare say you don't deserve it. If you'd rather not wear a ring that belonged to someone else, we can get another one."

"No, no, I'd be honored to wear your mother's ring."

"And you forgive me for laughing at you?"

"If you'll forgive me for being too sensitive and expecting you to read my mind."

"I think I can manage that."

They stopped talking long enough to kiss, and Phoebe swore it was the sweetest kiss she'd ever tasted. She might have enjoyed kissing him like that the rest of the afternoon—with the sun warming her pool-chilled skin and the smell of chlorine and Wyatt's aftershave tickling her nose—but a strange sound nibbled at the edges of her consciousness.

Wyatt must have heard it, too, because he pulled back and looked around.

They were being given a round of applause. Dozens of their neighbors were on their patios and balconies, clapping as if they'd just witnessed a bravura opera performance. She saw Elise and James, Daisy, her mother and Frannie, Jeff, Bill, the college girls—everybody she knew, just about.

She felt her face flaming, but she was laughing, too. "What a story for our grandchildren."

Wyatt seemed completely unfazed. "I love you, Phoebe."

"I love you, too. So much it hurts."

"Then let's take this show somewhere more private and…celebrate."

Phoebe was all for that.

Epilogue

The following weekend, Phoebe was dragged out of a lovely, deep sleep by the sound of strange voices. She opened her eyes, and it took her a moment to remember where she was.

Wyatt's bed.

Oh, how lovely, she thought. It was barely dawn, and neither she nor Wyatt had a thing to do today. Lots more hours to laze in bed. But then the voices came through again.

"Shh! We don't want to wake Wyatt," a woman said. Phoebe quickly realized it was Helen Madison!

"You don't think he'll be pleased when he finds out we took an earlier flight home?" Rolland asked. "We saved him a trip to the airport."

"At six-thirty on a Saturday morning, I doubt he'll be pleased about much of anything."

Her heart pounding, Phoebe punched Wyatt. "Wyatt! Wake up," she whispered urgently.

"Huh?"

"Your grandparents are home!"

"No, no," he said groggily. "I'm not supposed to pick them up until two this afternoon."

"Well, they're here! They must have taken a taxi."

Wyatt woke up all the way. He sat up, glanced at the clock, then out the window, and finally at Phoebe. "They're home?" He had that look in his eye, sort of like a deer in headlights.

"Do you want coffee, Rolland?" Helen asked. "Maybe the smell will wake Wyatt up."

"He doesn't like coffee, dear, remember?"

"Oh, right."

Panic welled up in Phoebe's chest. "What do we do? There's no way I can sneak out."

He put his arms around her and nuzzled her ear. "You don't have to sneak out. My grandparents will understand. We're engaged, after all."

"They told me to be nice to you. They didn't mean *this* nice."

"Oh, you'd be surprised what they might have meant. They've wanted us to get together for years."

"But not naked! Not in their guest room!"

Wyatt sighed and swung his feet over the side of the bed. "Okay, okay. I'll take them out on the balcony and show them how well I've been taking care of their plants. You sneak out the front door."

Phoebe jumped out of bed and frantically threw on clothes. Wyatt dressed in a more leisurely fashion, a faint smile on his face.

"You're enjoying this!" Phoebe accused.

"You're cute when you're panicked."

She huffed and shoved her feet into sandals, wondering where she'd left her purse. Well, she'd worry about that later.

Wyatt quickly kissed her. "I'll call you in a few

minutes to come over for coffee. Together we can share our good news with them.''

Phoebe's stomach fluttered. She loved the Madisons like her very own grandparents, but she wasn't sure how they would feel about her taking over their adored grandson.

''They'll be thrilled,'' Wyatt said, giving her one more quick kiss before exiting the room.

Phoebe listened through the cracked door as Wyatt welcomed Rolland and Helen. She felt warm all over as she heard the love they felt for each other, evidenced in their affectionate greeting. She couldn't wait to be part of this wonderful family. On top of the new understanding she and Olga had come to, she felt truly blessed.

She was so happy, in fact, that she wanted everyone to enjoy the same bliss. But so far Daisy was still alone. Then there were Frannie and Bill. Phoebe knew they truly cared for one another, but Frannie was still nursing her hurt feelings and Bill was certain he'd done nothing to warrant her cold shoulder.

''Let's go out on the balcony,'' she heard Wyatt say to his grandparents. ''The cactus is blooming.''

''Which one?'' Helen asked excitedly. ''The pink or the yellow?''

''Both.''

''Did you talk to them?''

''I did, but they didn't start blooming until I got stern with them….'' Their voices faded away.

Phoebe took a deep breath, darted down the hall and made for the front door. She realized as she reached for the knob that her keys were in her misplaced purse, but she supposed she could hang out with one of her other neighbors for a while.

"Don't you need this, Phoebe?"

Phoebe whirled around, her heart in her throat, to see Helen standing in the living room holding Phoebe's purse, a big smile on her face.

"How...what..." Phoebe's face burned. "Didn't you want to see the cactus?"

"I came back in to find my glasses. Don't look so stricken, dear. I already knew about you and Wyatt."

"How?"

"We ran into Frannie on our way into the building. She couldn't wait to spill the beans. We couldn't be happier. And don't worry, I remember what it was like to be young and in love." Helen stepped closer and handed Phoebe her purse. "Run home, now. I'll pretend like I never saw you."

Phoebe gave her a quick hug. "I think of you as my grandmother, you know."

"Well, I try. I'm sorry you didn't know your real grandma very well. But trust me when I say she would have been very happy to see you settled with Wyatt. She liked Wyatt."

"Wyatt knew my grandmother?"

Helen nodded. "I think that might be why she left you her condo in her will. She and I, well, we always thought the two of you might make a good couple."

"Why, you schemers!"

The French doors from the balcony opened, and Rolland stepped inside. "Helen? Can't you find your— oh, hello, Phoebe."

"Phoebe stopped in for coffee," Helen said smoothly, taking Phoebe's arm as if she'd just arrived.

She picked up her glasses from an end table where she'd left them, and they all joined Wyatt outside. He looked slightly surprised to see Phoebe, but he didn't hesitate to slip an arm around her and draw her next to him on the picnic table bench where he sat.

"I guess now's as good a time as any to tell you guys there've been a few changes while you were away...."

Phoebe sat back and let Wyatt enjoy breaking the joyful news, even though she knew Rolland and Helen already knew. Her happiness bloomed, just the way Helen's prickly cactus had bloomed when it got the right amounts of sun, water, love and a stern talking-to.

* * * * *

*Harlequin truly does
make any time special. . . .
This year we are celebrating
weddings in style!*

A Walk Down the Aisle
WEDDING CELEBRATION

To help us celebrate, we want you to tell us how wearing the Harlequin wedding gown will make your wedding day special. As the grand prize, Harlequin will offer one lucky bride the chance to **"Walk Down the Aisle"** in the Harlequin wedding gown!

There's more...

For her honeymoon, she and her groom will spend five nights at the **Hyatt Regency Maui.** As part of this five-night honeymoon at the hotel renowned for its romantic attractions, the couple will enjoy a candlelit dinner for two in Swan Court, a sunset sail on the hotel's catamaran, and duet spa treatments.

Maui • Molokai • Lanai

A HYATT RESORT AND SPA

To enter, please write, in, 250 words or less, how wearing the Harlequin wedding gown will make your wedding day special. The entry will be judged based on its emotionally compelling nature, its originality and creativity, and its sincerity. This contest is open to Canadian and U.S. residents only and to those who are 18 years of age and older. There is no purchase necessary to enter. Void where prohibited. See further contest rules attached. Please send your entry to:

Walk Down the Aisle Contest

In Canada	In U.S.A.
P.O. Box 637	P.O. Box 9076
Fort Erie, Ontario	3010 Walden Ave.
L2A 5X3	Buffalo, NY 14269-9076

You can also enter by visiting www.eHarlequin.com
Win the Harlequin wedding gown and the vacation of a lifetime!
The deadline for entries is October 1, 2001.

HARLEQUIN®
Makes any time special ®

PHWDACONT1

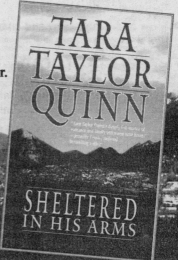

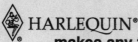

HARLEQUIN®
makes any time special—online...

eHARLEQUIN.com

shop eHarlequin

- ♥ Find all the new Harlequin releases at everyday great discounts.
- ♥ Try before you buy! Read an excerpt from the latest Harlequin novels.
- ♥ Write an online review and share your thoughts with others.

reading room

- ♥ Read our Internet exclusive daily and weekly online serials, or vote in our interactive novel.
- ♥ Talk to other readers about your favorite novels in our Reading Groups.
- ♥ Take our Choose-a-Book quiz to find the series that matches you!

authors' alcove

- ♥ Find out interesting tidbits and details about your favorite authors' lives, interests and writing habits.
- ♥ Ever dreamed of being an author? Enter our Writing Round Robin. The Winning Chapter will be published online! Or review our writing guidelines for submitting your novel.

All this and more available at
www.eHarlequin.com
on Women.com Networks